BED-
BUGS

COPYRIGHT © 2025 Martina Vidaić
TRANSLATION COPYRIGHT © 2025 Ellen Elias-Bursać
Originally published in Croatia as *Stjenice* by Ljevak in 2021.
DESIGN & LAYOUT Nikša Eršek
PUBLISHED BY Sandorf Passage
South Portland, Maine, United States
IMPRINT OF Sandorf
Severinska 30, Zagreb, Croatia
sandorfpassage.org
PRINTED BY Kerschoffset, Zagreb

Sandorf Passage books are available to the
trade through Independent Publishers Group:
ipgbook.com | (800) 888-4741.

Library of Congress Control Number: 2024953129

ISBN: 978-9-53351-538-0

Also available as an ebook;
ISBN: 978-9-53351-539-7

This book is published with financial support by the
Republic of Croatia's Ministry of Culture and Media.

Martina Vidaić
BED BUGS

translated by **ELLEN ELIAS-BURSAĆ**

SAN-
DORF
PAS-
SAGE

SOUTH PORTLAND | MAINE

I'M WRITING TO you, Hladna, my cold friend, because I happen to know you're the only person who won't laugh when I say that the day the ants chewed holes in my underwear, I finally had to face up to the fact that my downfall was a certainty. As if there in that laundry bag with the dirty clothes, where the ants—hunkering down with their nibbling—trembled with dark, gaping maws, something long obvious was articulated in the most unpleasant way possible. I see you now, as I always do, as if sketched with quick strokes of brown chalk against the white background of the infirmary, as you briefly shut your eyes and press them with your right thumb and index finger, as you always do when something doesn't quite make sense; then, you prop your leg up on the desk and light a cigarette without moving your eyes from my letter, and your whole face focuses on the tip of your nose, which you tweak nervously and playfully, as if it holds all the answers. A late spring afternoon. Have you already turned on the lights, or are you squinting in the gloom? Maybe you have a glass of pelin bitters on the table, which every so often you bring to your lips. Do drink. You'll need it—the moment has finally come for you to learn who I am, or at least who I am when nobody sees me. You probably know what ants are like: they foretell calamities. They showed up in my bag of dirty laundry after one calamity had already happened—the car crash. Nearly half a year had passed by then since the crash, and my sick leave had been used up months before, but I didn't go back to work. First Igor tried calling; then he sent me emails, texts, messages over Viber and WhatsApp, official letters by snail mail, phone messages via his secretary. Meanwhile, I was sitting in my darkened apartment, either on the couch or at the kitchen table, perspiring in the viscous August air, staring at my laptop, two phones, and tablet, lining them up one next to the other as if they'd been confiscated in a police raid—and I was stuck. I hardly dared so much as touch the other things in the apartment, as if they were there on loan, still wrapped in that sense of decorum that compels us to use them gingerly and only when needed. This must be confusion resulting from the amnesia, you'll say, from those few minutes before the crash that have been lost forever. But what you don't know is far more important: that gap of a few minutes ripped my life in two, and oddly pushed away everything that had come before it. What I could remember of my life, perhaps even more clearly than before, was indeed my past, but it felt alien, like the way I might recall a movie or a TV series. I could reconstruct with crystalline precision the events down to the finest detail, but I was no longer inside the experience. How can I respond to the messages they're sending me, how can I do this job that is supposedly mine, when my very name sounds alien to me, imposed, almost as if it isn't a name a human being ought to have? I was able, though only barely, to get up, lie down, bring food from the grocery store to the kitchen, eat, repeat the most basic rituals of hygiene, and wait for something undetermined, in an unending state of nervous boredom, as if on vacation in a dreary apartment in a dismal city while it rains and there's nothing to do, and every attempt at starting something—if nothing else, at least reading a book or listening to music—reminds me unpleasantly that my time is limited and soon will be up. I lived that way for months, refusing to respond, justifying my absence with the occasional text message. And I avoided visits to you, hiding behind pathetic excuses. What was I hoping for? Did I still actually think somebody would come knocking on my door, make me let them in, and then—embraced once more by human arms—I'd find myself? If I ever believed in something like that, the ants devoured my belief down to the last nibble. The ants were minuscule, weirdly speedy, a kind I hadn't seen since coming to live in Zagreb, though I'd studied them closely as a child. With savage greed they chomped the stains of marmalade, sauce, fruit—or ooze—chewing right through the stain and the cloth it was on. When I opened the laundry bag to put fourteen, as I later counted, of the fifteen panties I owned into the wash, the damage I found was already beyond repair. All I could do was submerge the ants in water and throw the gnawed panties into the trash. They also destroyed two blouses and a skirt, but there were other blouses and skirts to be had, while panties I needed to buy. I sat down to have a think about this. My funds were already running low. I had enough to pay my rent and bills for the next month and live frugally until the first autumn rains, which I was looking forward to as if the rains were going to serve as a magic haven. I don't know what I was expecting, what sort of salvation would come raining down upon me from the sky. Perhaps I believed that when the first cold front dispelled the humidity that had soaked up the full burden of this year, I'd move on to a fresh frame of mind and I'd know exactly what needed doing. I'm thinking now that maybe I'd been waiting my whole life for this fresh frame of mind. But it cannot come, can it, Hladna? Isn't the future a fiction in which we're outside our body, while the present is a reality where we return, ruthlessly, every morning, over and over, to our body, to our neck's dull ache, our sweaty armpits, painful hangnails, ingrown hairs, discharge gnawed by ants, leaving us short of panties? Sorry, I bet I'm boring you with all these silly questions. Now you're probably on your second or third pelin; maybe you even brought out the whole bottle, because you can tell this is getting serious. You turn on the lamp and it casts a golden glow over your face, and this gives you a perky look but also highlights the fact that you haven't washed your hair. Can you hear the birds in the bush under the window? No, sorry, no more questions. Just answers. Yes, I answer, I bought myself a pair of panties. Black, with little white hearts. Along with the ones I was wearing at the time of the ant attack, white with little black hearts. Now I had two pairs. Each evening I'd take one off, dip it in hot water, scrub it with soap, and leave it out on the windowsill to dry. I was afraid to leave dirty panties in the laundry bag till morning, for fear the ants might attack again, requiring a wasteful expense on yet another new pair, and I'd never make it to those autumnal rains.

By any means necessary, I needed to defend my remaining panties. Whenever I turned out the light, the patter of billions of tiny feet filled the room from floor to ceiling. Dense, heavy, and nervously painful, they teemed into all my orifices—my nostrils and mouth, vagina and anus, belly button, ears, under my nails and eyelids—and then gnawed at my internal organs with such gusto that I was afraid to sleep, quaking that by morning nothing but an empty shell would be left of me. One night at the very end of August, they were particularly loathsome. In waves they surged from the ceiling, and in an entirely unpredictable order they touched me with broad swings of their minuscule, sharp pincers—now this part of the body, now that part—as if toying. I felt myself burn, but whenever I touched a spot where they had just been, the skin was clammy and unpleasantly sticky. I turned on the light, not realizing that vestiges of the ominous darkness would continue lurking under my panties and tank tops. I stripped them off too, but the dark had pooled in my bodily crevices and under my hairs. My hair follicles would not stop itching. I raised the blinds and planted myself on my elbows by the open window. The night was pitch-black, quiet the way creatures are quiet when they have something to hide. Not a single star in the sky; the windows facing my window on all three sides of the courtyard were shrouded or dark, and there was no sign of the usual glints of light off the chassis and headlights of the cars parked below. It's those ants, I thought; the yard is seething with them, and there's no way out. From the dark nooks of my body, they summoned the night into the apartment to smother me. I didn't try lowering the blinds. I sat on the windowsill and stared dully into the blind darkness that was stirring impatiently. Then it happened. In the distance, a quick flash. Then another. For a few long moments—nothing. And finally: a vast, blazing fissure at the very heart of the darkness thundered with a magnificent racket. Furious rain began to pelt, and I burst into tears for the first time since the crash. Through the tears I laughed. A storm, I whispered, it's just a storm, knucklehead. Back I went to bed and fell peacefully asleep for the first time in a week. The next day the sun came out, but no longer was the air humid. I raised all the blinds and opened the windows wide. The fresh air, I couldn't get enough, and it seemed to be demanding that now was the time to clean and clean and clean. So, I cleaned. Not only the obvious places, like dusting the shelves, brushing crumbs from the rug, and scrubbing the scaling from the toilet and kitchen and the stains from the floor, but much more thoroughly, deeper and further: the tops of the wardrobes, the dark backs behind the framed pictures, the coldest corner of the refrigerator, the sensitive fluting on the table lamps, the keyholes and hinges on the windows, all the way to the deepest depths of the shoe cabinet. I inhaled with pleasure the smell of the cleaning fluids I was slathering on so generously. I'll eradicate those ants, I told myself, down to the very last larva, plug every hole, blow a cloud of poison into each passageway that will bust their little heads if they so much as think of coming near me. I bet you're wondering where this attack of optimism could have come from, when I'd already written that I finally realized, at the sight of the ants devouring my underwear, that my downfall was a certainty. True, I did realize this, but generally a person fiercely denies what she knows best. And when you find yourself in a spotless, pristine apartment full of intimate pale-blue sky, prevarication comes easily. I don't know if I've ever told you about the place where I was living. It was quiet, well lit, in a small building facing an inner courtyard on Medveščak, and comfortable when the sun wasn't beating down too harshly, with furnishings provided by the landlord, five tolerably bad pictures, but two cute table lamps with rectangular shades that gave the room a somewhat moderate, elegant warmth, and all the odds and ends I had brought with me: the books and ornamental boxes, the red rope bowl with a decorative silver anchor where I kept fruit, the yellow wire dish that held candies. I had houseplants on the windowsill, cactuses on the shoe cabinet, a green tablecloth with purple flowers, curtains that resembled spaghetti, a tufted hassock and baby-blue covers on the pillows, on which the hot-yellow triangles sometimes seemed to be cavorting with glee. In places like this you may find it easy to accept the feeling that you're living in a lifestyle magazine article. The successful thirty-five-year-old architect sits in her charmingly furnished apartment on Medveščak, and after an enjoyable day of cleaning and cooking, she has her feet up on the hassock and is listening to jazz playing on her turntable, while still savoring the flavors of the spinach spread on rounds of toast and the squash soup, the salad of carrots, raisins, and almonds, and the juicy duck with a side of millet and vegetables, all reminding her of how merciful the world can be. Then the successful architect's phone rings. How does she react? you might ask. How is the woman going to deal with a ringing phone, when for months she hasn't responded to a single call? This time I did pick up, I'm telling you, the way one does when one's phone rings, swiping the finger reflexively across the screen where the unknown number pulses and bringing the phone casually to the ear. But as soon as I heard the woman's voice on the other end, I knew I shouldn't have. Not that I knew her voice, but something about it rocked the stability of the day, a little like a hurtling roller coaster at an amusement park that trundles steadily along over level stretches of track, going either up or down, but when it reaches a curve it does an abrupt, out-of-control jolt that tricks you into thinking the whole train is about to veer off and plunge downward—an impression lingering for a few seconds above the heads of those who are watching the whole thing from below, though obviously it won't. The jolt was already there in the word *evening* of the phrase *good evening*, and when the woman asked whether she was speaking with Gorana Hrabrov, there was a jolt for me in hearing this name, which was, supposedly, still mine. With the combination of pride and arrogance typical of widows of Yugoslav People's Army officers, she announced her own name, firmly fixed in palatals that she spat out as if hammering in nails with the breath from her mouth, and when she explained, after a brief pause, that she was Sergej's mother, there was the jolt in Sergej's name. Hladna, you may remember Sergej, my, well, my husband. "We've not had the opportunity to meet," said Sergej's mother, "but Sergej told me so much about you over the phone during the brief time you were together, and he said only the nicest things." She declared this quite seriously, without a trace of irony, but the jolts gave the words a tinge of slipperiness. I felt a surge of icy malaise, as I always did when someone's intentions made no sense to me. "And then that terrible accident," she said, "*that* terrible, terrible accident took him from us." Shaken, I closed my eyes and listened in the dark to her muffled sobs. I tried to picture her, but into my mind's eye instead floated Sergej's saintly visage, as if composed of triangles cut from a nonliving substance—wax or pale plastic—and with his too lively, nearly impossible eyes, blue in such a violent way that the skin around them took on an enduring martyr's dark-gray hue. Only his head of unruly black hair was elusive, from which a lock escaped at times from my awareness like a shy little snake. The way his mother was present on the phone, bolstered by her outdated sense of privilege as an army widow, summoned Sergej to the darkness, and now it is suddenly him I'm seeing—neatly combed, his hair tamed with oil and parted down the middle—sitting there with the phone to his ear, sobbing softly, with dignity. "I do hope he didn't suffer," says this Sergej. "I just hope he didn't suffer," says Sergej again. How can I respond? What can I say, when I no longer even know for sure that my name is my name? I clearly remember our brief relationship, how he and I met at the symposium, the high-speed wedding, the crazy drive we called our honeymoon along the Brotherhood and Unity Highway, and then our return along the same road, dry as could be, up to a few minutes before the crash in Lika on the 19 February 2019, at seven o'clock in the morning. I remember it all—his pointy snakeskin shoes and our rings from chocolate Kinder eggs, and the fat saleslady at the gas station in Ilok—but I don't know what it all meant. Who was Sergej to me? I was tempted to tell his mother I hadn't seen Sergej dead, and often a person cannot know what another person really means to them until the person's crushed skull tells them, but I managed to control myself and said I couldn't remember the crash and was still searching for answers, and I, too, earnestly hoped he hadn't suffered. I said this last part so unconvincingly, with the emphasis all wrong on *earnestly*, which gave the sentence an almost ironic twist, that she was quiet for a moment and I thought she'd hung up. Instead, she sobbed again, now a little louder. I don't know how to respond to people when they cry; it can make me feel as if I am coming toward them with a frying pan full of sizzling oil, and while the warmth may save them, I must take care that no tears drop into the hot oil and spray our faces. I felt my phone sliding from my hand, slippery with sweat. "He was always a rebel, but I never held that against him. I don't hold anything against you kids," Sergej's mother said with conviction, but as she passed through the jolt of *kids*, the dislocation glared. We were hardly kids, as could be felt in what she said; we were two crazies who drove straight into death. I gave a fake little laugh, quick and creepy. "Sergej must have been bright as a kid," I hazarded. This hooked her. Her voice mildly warmed. Oh, so bright, he knew his multiplication tables even before he started school. He learned to write when he was four. At five he read the newspaper with his grandfather. "Aha," I said. At ten he was reading books on political economics by Edvard Kardelj and debating self-management socialism with his father. In spirit he was a democrat. At twelve, a punk rocker. "Aha," I said. At the age of six he criticized his grandmother for the nutritional poverty of her cooking. He knew all the capital cities of the world, all the rivers, even the smallest ones. He read Shakespeare, Dostoevsky, and Krleža before he finished primary school. "Aha," I said. There were no jolts or dislocations in what she was saying, and it sounded as if the amusement park train ride of Sergej's early achievements would trundle on and on and on; instead, the jolts had moved into the final "a" in each *aha* I issued, and the whole composition of our conversation was dangerously rocking. She must have felt this, because she stopped speaking. What followed was an uncomfortable but welcome pause. "I'm afraid I'll have to go; work is calling," I said with relief. "Yes, yes, of course, dear, of course," she replied, shaken, with only a little of her initial confidence, her tone that of an elderly woman who would be left alone in dark silence. And, so, we finished. But you know how it goes, some conversations don't end where they end. I tried sitting back down on my pristine couch, nibbling at chocolate and listening to *In A Silent Way*, but all in vain. The couch had two tiny holes in the armrest; there were a few drops of red wine on the upholstered legs that I couldn't scrub off. The ceiling had ever so slightly yellowed in the corners, the household plants were dotted with dry leaves, and there was nothing left to be done about the tassels on the rug. I grabbed my laptop and googled obsessively for an hour, not sure, myself, of what I was after. Everything the internet could tell me about Sergej and his family I already knew. An only child in a Belgrade officer's family, a singer in several punk bands, a degree in theology, an amateur painter. Two hours later, the same: only child, singer, theologian, painter. And again around midnight. And at 2 a.m. At 4 a.m. I suddenly thought, for no particular reason, of the mornings when I was a little girl and got up before first light to go out with my parents and work in the fields, planting or harvesting potatoes and onions. Getting out of bed was like wriggling out

BEDBUGS 15

from under a heavy stone slab, and in the evening the exhaustion, too, was slablike, and sleep came on like a quick swoon. That deep, dreamless sleep is probably the closest thing I've known to death, but perhaps because the nights were like death, the days pulsed with unadulterated life, ready in its immediacy. The soil offered friendly resistance when I pressed in the potatoes, the birds openly flaunted their intention to work against us, and my father's hands—his old, peasant fingers with nails that could no longer be scrubbed clean, greasy from the bacon he sliced and fed me during our lunch breaks—were truly a parent's hands. You might say, Hladna, I should have been glad that my ability to experience was finally coming back. Maybe it was back, but this filled me with anxiety. I sat on the rented couch at four in the morning, exhausted from the hours of pointless googling, and the weariness I felt was not like the weight of a stone slab but more like an irritating, chafing cataract in my eye. There was no difference between weighty and weightless. Does that make sense? My feeling of exhaustion was nothing but an irritating, calloused apathy. Why am I wasting my life like this, why don't I do something? I plagued myself with questions, but with no real will to find any answers. A fitful sleep only overtook me at around five. When I woke at noon and noticed the first bedbug bite, I couldn't work up much alarm. Something was bound to happen, so why not this. I still hadn't figured out that this was a bedbug invasion; the red spot on the middle finger of my right hand, slightly swollen and painful, easily could have passed for an ordinary mosquito bite, though right away I had an inkling this might be different. After the most recent citywide spraying, there had been no buzzing of mosquitoes for several days, and the bite was not just itchy, it hurt. Only that evening, when identical red dots formed a straight line on the fingers, but not the thumb, of the same hand, did I have to admit I had never been bitten by a mosquito quite like that. These were clearly bites of a different sort: on the red swells I could see something slightly darker, a tiny point, the place where the proboscis had pierced the skin. If they weren't mosquitoes, what were they? Once more I went to Google and Google told me: bedbugs. Not only that. Google said: once they get into an apartment, bedbugs are extremely difficult to get rid of. They do not react to regular household cleansers, but only to very high temperatures. They lodge in the joints of furniture and the cracks in the parquet flooring, where they lay eggs that sometimes survive even the most rigorous treatments. Professional pest control is needed to eradicate them, and sometimes even that won't do it. Evacuation may be required. Furniture may have to be replaced. A complete renovation of the apartment might be in order. For the first time, I felt something like panic. This was not a moment when I could afford professional pest control, and the idea that I should ask my landlord to pay for it was doubly unacceptable: apparently, I had somehow introduced these bedbugs, and the last thing I wanted was for my landlord—a young businessman with a phone glued to his ear, about whom what I liked best was that I never saw him—to start hanging around. And besides, in addition to the cost, I quaked at the very idea of having to move out of the apartment. The six months I had been here were my emotional history, a history that was mine alone. I could not bear the thought of strangers setting foot in my history. Besides, where would I go? A call to the very people I'd been refusing to see for months felt like madness, as if I were stopping a random passerby and asking to be allowed to move in with them over the holidays. This was something I would have to deal with on my own. The next morning, I threw myself into an energetic vacuuming of the whole place, focusing on the couch and the bed, which I finished, following Google's instructions, by throwing the vacuum bags into the trash and taking the trash bag out to the dumpster. I disassembled the couch and bed and heated each part with my hair dryer. I spent three days washing and drying my clothes, and vacuum-packed the delicate items for a three-week quarantine. Only when I'd finished with all of this did I start to feel pain radiating through my muscles and bones and hear an unfamiliar crunching sound in my spine. For the first time in my life, I caught myself thinking: I'm getting old. My right hand still itched unbearably, especially at night, and was constantly swollen, but no new red dots appeared. My fingers looked disgusting—fat yellow worms, because, as I had no antibiotics, I'd smeared them with a paste made of turmeric and water. There were moments when I wondered what would happen if the condition became so acute that I needed medical help, but I quickly did my best to squelch those thoughts. I'd lost my health coverage after Igor fired me, and I hadn't yet registered for unemployment, but this fact only now found its way into my body, transforming it into a precious, fragile being with whose care I had been entrusted and whose mysterious whims might be life-threatening. With each thought of the doctors I couldn't turn to, the medical terms we use to talk about our bodies fled from me, and this loss led me down into a dangerous rabbit hole: loneliness in its most absolute form. On the other hand, the apartment was experiencing a transformation of a different sort. There were no visible signs of the bedbugs' presence, maybe because in that earlier cleaning, before Sergej's mother called, I had inadvertently removed all possible traces of their dot-shaped feces and had laundered sheets that might have had bloody stains on them. No, there was no proof, no sweetish smell exuding from the couch and bed, but the process of transforming the space, begun right after the call from Sergej's mother, now intensified. There were so many cracks in the parquet flooring and on the wooden furniture, which, at first glance, had seemed to be simple. The couch feigned a beige gentility only to conceal the inner decrepitude of its springs. And the pictures on the wall, how they watched me with their quasi-innocent pastel flowers, long since caked with dust. The apartment, now I knew this, was colluding with the bedbugs, permitting them to move in by offering no resistance. Day after day, while the condition of my right hand remained unchanged, I found this treachery increasingly difficult to bear. I began wandering off for long, aimless evening rambles. I went to New Zagreb, Jarun, Vrapče, Mirogoj, or Maksimir, seeking the periphery of the city, the parts of town where the buildings and passersby were few and far between, where my thoughts could be out in the open air. But the first early September nocturnal chill left me feeling alone with my throbbing fingers. This sent me back to the neighborhoods where the city was more densely populated, and the heavy, sooty facades and pedestrians settled pleasantly upon my mind, thanks to the trams slicing across the streets, at any moment threatening to fold them like sheets of paper. I love observing the city, the way it is always irreversibly changing. Always different people in always different places. This soothed me. Bedbugs, too, are transient, are they not? I was pleased when I noticed things I hadn't spotted before: a tree growing on a balcony, the glow of an orange light inside a tailor's shop, or a sign in the window of a boutique. Perhaps there are good design ideas out there, I thought, they just haven't been picked up yet. I particularly liked looking at the windows. My favorites were the old wood-framed windows, the ones with both an outside window with leaves swinging outward and an inside window with leaves swinging inward, a wide sill between them. The stodgy, cloaked air of Austro-Hungarian buildings allowed itself a flash of vulnerability with them, at once both transparent and concealing. The outer window aired its vulnerability, while the inner one, half hidden behind flowers or curtains, suggested something more, and together they allowed for an openly stated truth while also questioning that same truth. If ever I design buildings again, I thought, my first building will have those old-fashioned double windows. Yes, the architect in me must be stirring and engaging face-to-face with the city. But whenever I crept into the courtyard of my building on Medveščak, the two PVC windows on the second floor looked down on me with their dark panes, blinkered and impenetrable, the blinds slightly lowered as if my presence irked them, and I felt as if I were returning to the wrong place where I'd have to spend yet another night with the bedbugs. Still, I slept well on those nights, perhaps too well. Only occasionally did I wake up before morning, turn on the lamp, and start hunting for them. Never a one. The boats in one of the pictures seemed weirdly frozen, as if they had only come to shore a moment before, yet were pretending to have been there all along. The half-naked woman in the other picture turned her profile to me, refusing to say where the bedbugs were taking my blood. Never a single shred of evidence. But a week after the first bites, a new line of red dots appeared, this time on the fingers of my left hand. I forced myself not to panic, but part of the ease with which I fended off the panic included gradual surrender. Again, I went through the cleaning, heating, and scrubbing, but not half as thoroughly as I had the first time. It seemed pointless to waste my last stores of detergents, so this time I washed only the clothes I'd touched or worn recently, and only scrubbed the outer surfaces of the couch and bed, because I spent my stamina too fast. I felt silly, as if there were a big bedbug in the sky, looking down from above, mocking my efforts, and the walls and pictures and wardrobe and couch and bed and all my clothes were slyly joining in on the fun. After all this, there was no longer any satisfaction with a job well done—only rage and impotence giving rise to a reflexive urge to weep with sobs like hacking coughs. I was on the verge of banging my head against the wall. So, I called Maria. Have I mentioned Maria, my older sister? You might well point out that all my sisters are older, and indeed they are, but she's the eldest—over sixty. You know her; she's the one who married Omer and had to move to Ljubljana so the lopsidedness of their names—his Muslim, hers Croatian—could find a balance. I don't know why I called her, of all people. I hadn't spoken with her since New Year's and hadn't seen her in over two years. There was something, I guess, in the rage and impotence and the urge to sob that reminded me of her. Maybe this had to do with the time when I was five and a tall blond boy, the village bully, explained, in a tone both serious and alarming, that my mother was much too old to be my mother—with a crowd of local kids smirking at me from behind him—while my nephews and nieces, all of them around my age, said not a word and kicked pebbles around until Maria came over and explained to everyone that I had the upper hand because I was the only one who had nephews and nieces, and then she sent us all home, not forgetting to wink at me in passing. The taunting by the other kids must have filled me with rage and impotence, right? Or did the rage and impotence come along later, after Maria intervened, because I couldn't bear it that my sister was treating me like I was her kid? Now, when she greeted me over the phone as if we'd been chatting daily, I tried to remember how I saw the tall blond boy after he was sent home. I remember him leering at me as he left, but what did the leer mean to me? If I found him to be confused and ashamed, shot down, perhaps I loved Maria all the more for her intervention and was now calling her in search of comfort. But if I saw his leer as a kind of riddle, out of reach, coming from someone who knew more about me than I knew about myself, then maybe that moment shaped my view of myself, and I seldom called Maria on the phone because she'd been permanently tagged in my subconscious as someone who had chosen to console me with lies. I trembled at this possibility, thinking how, now that I was, indeed, calling her, I'd be able to explain why. Luckily, she didn't ask. As if talking to herself, she rattled on for minutes, hours, days about Omer, Martina, Rina, and Sara and several of her friends. Omer was spending his days puttering with model ships, what else could he do, he'd given his heart and soul to his job at Elektra. Martina was still working as an attorney for Social Services, not that she couldn't have done better, but she had to stick with it for the kids. Rina was vegan and living on a commune, whatever that was, on a farm near Ljubljana and was all caught up in Zen Buddhism. Sara, now isn't this just like Sara, was racing from one sport to another, from one university department to another. It felt good to let Maria prattle on, just as it had felt good to watch people walking through the city. Though Maria found something major or minor to gripe about, she didn't actually sound snide or grumpy. Her overbright, high-pitched voice was not capable of producing credible malaise; she turned everything into jolly, bouncy fun. At first, I enjoyed this. But after a while her voice created a light-filled space, and anything seriously dark was impossible to introduce or sustain longer than the time needed to get the words out, certainly not long enough to hold her attention. It was impossible for me to say: "Sister, dear, the bedbugs are going to eat me alive if you don't help." I felt a surge of bile. I recalled how Maria, as far back as I could remember, spoke with others in our family as if she'd always had the Slovenian language in her ear, interfering with her Croatian, justifying her small yet key lack of comprehension. Might she be using the same ploy with me now? Maybe the way she pitched her voice high was a deliberate conceit. Maybe she knew I wasn't well and was taking care to keep my frame of mind from becoming so obvious that she would be unable to ignore it. Having thought this, I was consumed by a desire to mock her. I repeated every word she was saying, changing each one ever so slightly to pile on the irony. But, swayed, I guess, by the same overpowering brightness that her voice introduced, my voice also took on a cheery, impenetrable tone, without the dark chasm irony requires, like the chasm a tightrope walker needs in order to appear daring. Everything I said sounded as if I were overjoyed. My joy was so compelling that by the end of our conversation, I had actually begun feeling glad. My life was problem-free. And after we finished, the giddy feeling of glee kept its hold on me until I began transitioning to sheer stupor. It was as if I couldn't remember how I'd gotten there and what I needed. To do something for myself, I took a book off the shelf, sat at the desk, and tried to read. The book was by Stephen Hawking, about his popular theory of physics, one of the few I'd read over the last half year, but now I couldn't get beyond the first sentence. I switched on the lamp, the smaller one atop the chest of drawers next to my desk. True, there was still daylight, a late September afternoon, but the sky, the generous slice of it I could see through the rooftops, was dark gray with clouds. I switched off the lamp. It is still daytime, I thought, but the shadow of the sky is creeping in and looming darker than before. I reached again for the switch, pressed it—and recoiled when, after a brief flash, there was a popping sound and the light did not come on. Incredulous, I quickly pressed the switch several times. Nothing. Just the opaque lampshade. The insidious treachery of a lightbulb. You are the only one who won't laugh, Hladna, when I tell you there can be no worse betrayal. That instant I knew what I'd do, but first, with all my might, I kicked the iron desk leg several times, and then, deliberately, almost solemnly, I yanked the plug of the electric cord out of the socket in a fury and threw the lamp into the middle of the room. Ha! Now that was true joy. Did you notice, Hladna, that in true joy there is always a little something bad? Do you think this is because there can be no real joy without real freedom? Well, this was freedom, that's for sure. I got up and stomped right foot left foot, right foot left foot, right foot left foot on the toppled rectangular lampshade, until all that was left of it was the twisted metal frame and tiny shreds of brown cloth, like crumbs of chocolate. That's what these old lamps are like, I thought, they never give up on being cute, even when it's all over. The thought filled me with shame. I quit stomping and retreated back to the couch, surveying what I'd done. From the apartment below I couldn't hear the usual nasal voices: the old man's that stretched like chewing gum, the old woman's like the sloshing of liquid in a barrel, or the puppylike whimpers of their grandchildren; they must have all stopped talking when they heard the racket. The whole room looked as if it were shaking, but when the feeling of the shaking subsided, the things around me assumed a terrible, petrified air of reproach. The blue-gray sky pressed in through the window. I staggered over to the desk, and in a drawer I found matches and the stub of a half-burned yellow candle that looked a lot like a disembodied thumb. I lit the wick. Was I aware of what I was about to do? Or did I really think after all this that I'd go on with my reading about theoretical physics? Hard to say, Hladna. I think I wasn't up to thinking. I let everything progress with a dull automatism. When the flame had melted enough wax, I dribbled some on the first sheet of paper I found and stuck the candle to the paper. And I did continue trying to read the book, but the reading was even more pointless than it had been the first time around.

Behind my back lay the remains of the lamp; a mute presence began to grow, reminding me of the way my dead father had been present, more than twenty years before, while we held our nocturnal vigil in our home. I may have imagined this, the feeling, yet now I understood far better why it is the dead are never left alone in a room. I didn't dare look at the corpse of the lamp, but I had to keep track of its presence so it wouldn't creep up on me. The time was about five o'clock in the afternoon, and the day looked as though it could no longer be budged from the spot. The dark sky sat in the window of the facing building and glared at me, motionless, with no less reproach than did the things in the apartment. Even the plants on the windowsill had something judgmental about them. My fingers hurt as I leafed through the pages, and with each passing minute they itched more. They looked silly, all swollen and red like plump little sausages. The more I scratched them, the more they itched, and the more the itch spread to other parts of my body. At that point, I changed into different clothes. I swear, Hladna, my only intention was to feel on my skin something lighter and cooler, something like rayon, something cold, like the name I call you. It was still summery. But, you'll ask, why did I choose that particular dress, which I had never worn around the apartment? Where was I thinking of going? I don't know. I'm telling you, everything happened as it did because events seemed preordained to happen that way. I believe what I had in mind was to vacuum up the fragments of the lamp, and for that I needed new vacuum bags, so I took my purse with my wallet, slipped on my sneakers, and headed for the door. At first, I forgot all about the candle. But then I stopped in the front hall and turned. I must have seen it through the partly open door between the kitchen and the living room. The gust of fresh air from the open hallway must have flickered the flame. I must have seen that, right? I think I did, but there still wasn't anything deliberate about my actions. I simply looked at the upright burning thumb, as if checking: gas, off; or lightbulb, off; or faucet, off. As if this were exactly as it was supposed to be as I was leaving the apartment. The same confusing automatism led me to step back in and tuck the panties that had been drying on the windowsill into my purse. Only when I slammed the door behind me and remembered that I'd left behind my keys for the special anti-theft lock, which, of course, cannot be opened from the outside, did I know that I would not be returning. It did occur to me that I could call the landlord and request another key, but the very idea felt far too complicated, something almost impossible to deal with in reality. And besides, all my communication devices were in there. For a few minutes, I stood there by the door, listening, and I'm not even sure what I was listening for. Then I simply walked away. Have you ever done anything totally outrageous, Hladna? Smashed a valuable vintage lamp to pieces, killed someone, set someone else's apartment on fire? They say in such moments a person feels alive as they'd never felt before. True, but not like you'd think. Not the way people feel who have evaded death by a hair: powerful, as if their body had been given back to them so they can rule it with greater sovereignty. No, there was no awareness here about my body. I felt—how can I put this—like an animal. By saying this, I'm not thinking of any remorse or self-reproach. I did not feel like a human being who was thinking: I am an animal. No, I actually *was* an animal. An animal in flight. And there were witnesses to my flight lurking at every window that faced the inner courtyard. One of the neighbors, a good-natured older man with whom I'd occasionally exchanged a few words, ran into me as he was leaving his storage unit. "Hello there, neighbor," he said, "where are you off to in such a rush?" My animal ear caught the tinge of a cooling of tone in the last word of his question. Had he picked up on something? "Might rain, do you think?" he went on, and his smile, because of a half-drooping eyelid, seemed sly. I noticed there were beads of sweat on his upper lip. I tried edging around him, mumbling a response. "But at least it's warm, there's that," he said through a chuckle resembling rolling gravel. He was burying me. The old man in his tattered undershirt, from which his seallike arms hung, only seemed to be inert at first glance. I wanted to push him away. "How do they say it where you're from in Dalmatia?" In one of the apartments somebody was brewing coffee; the scent of freshly washed laundry wafted from the balconies. People were existing. And they had eyes and ears and noses. I felt as if I'd start to smell burning paper at any moment. When he opened his mouth to say something more, I cut him off sharply and fled toward the courtyard door. I heard his surprised mumbling but didn't turn around. Witnesses were lurking behind every wall. I walked faster than I ever have in my life, nearly at a run, all the way to the main square, and then, with no plan at all, I hurried into a department store. Have I told you how I love those old-fashioned department stores? Something about them reminds me of the 1990s' New York of the movies. A wealth of choices so tastefully presented that you feel as if there could be no other choices, and yet you feel no pressure. The ease of the escalator. The aging salesmen and salesladies who are waiting for either their pensions or death. As soon as I went in, I felt, again, like a human being, or, at least, no longer like an animal. I briefly surveyed the cosmetics and shoes on the ground floor and then took the escalator to Women's Wear. I had no plan at all, like I said; I was just enjoying being in this space that exuded safety, wandering and sifting through clothing that I did not, actually, find at all appealing. I noticed a saleslady eyeing me. I didn't like the way she watched me, furtively, over racks of clothes, out of the corner of her eye, with an interest that suggested a hint of recognition. I became aware that my dress, with its tiny pale-blue and pale-yellow flowers, looked like a nightgown on me, untanned as I was. I began checking out the dark-colored dresses tailored with starker lines. I felt the saleslady move closer. The way she was doing this, silently, slowly, made me nervous. And when she said, "May I help you?" her soft voice, nearly at a whisper, shy and brimming with excessive respect, gave me the chills. Confused, I stammered something. This encouraged her. She stepped closer and gestured to dresses I hadn't yet had a look at. "Might these interest you?" she asked. Her voice cooled, lending her excessively respectful tone a false veneer. Clearly, she despised me. I saw this in her gray eyes, deeply inset in her pallid, doughy face. I'm telling you, Hladna, that woman had me pegged. I wanted to tell her I wasn't what she thought I was; there were circumstances I didn't fully recall or couldn't quite explain, and they had brought me to the point where my life was nearing its end. But instead, I broke out in a cold sweat and blushed crimson and readily agreed, the way a child accepts her punishment, to every dress she offered me. What was it that I so desperately wanted this woman to think of me? That I was a good girl? That I'm not what I looked like to her? I felt awkward about leaving the dressing room when a dress didn't suit me. I even agreed to try on ones I'd never buy in a million years. Maybe this wasn't about the saleslady at all. Maybe I simply had the chance to feel what it was like to be back among people, when something is expected of you. I finally purchased a simple knee-length black dress with three-quarter-length sleeves. When I asked her to remove the tag because I would be wearing the dress out of the store, she gave me a look but said nothing. She simply passed the cold scissors over the seam between the back and the neck, snipped the thread, and took my payment. I was about to say something to justify myself, but she had already moved on to the next customer. Chagrined, I went down to Shoes and bought a pair of the simplest black flats and stuffed my dirty white sneakers into the shopping bag with the old dress. On my way out, I dropped the bag into a trash bin. Then I went into the adjacent drugstore. This was one of those places where you can be made up for free if you buy what they're selling, so right away I sat in the chair and the makeup artist—a young woman whose unnaturally black hair was so painfully pulled back in a ponytail that her face looked like a rubber mask—began, wordlessly, to apply liquid powder to my face. She was expressionless, mildly invidious in her manner, not at all nervous, and slow, really, but a glance at her eyebrows, symmetrically drawn like swallows' wings in a children's drawing, filled me with dread. There were thousands of women in town whose eyebrows were drawn like these, and some of them were sure to be passing by the window of the drugstore at that very moment.

I could see them through the glass as they went down the street, heading west or east, and some were going all the way to Medveščak, walking right by the big, heavy wooden door that led into the courtyard of my apartment building. How long had I been at the department store? By now, the candle stub, short as it was, might have burned down. If it caught the paper, the wooden desk was already burning. In a flash the curtains would catch fire. Then the neighbors would notice. Or not. Evening had come, and outside the sky was dark. The fire might attract attention. But around the courtyard, the neighbors seldom noticed the things that mattered. Once the curtain rod falls, the apartment will be done for, I thought. Flames will engulf the rug, and then the couch, the parquet floor, and the door, and there will be no turning back. And hundreds of young women with eyebrows drawn like the makeup artist's will walk to the left and to the right; they will pass by fire stations and police stations, by insurance companies and my landlord's home up on Srebrnjak. I fidgeted in the chair, struggling to breathe—what with the particles of eye shadow and powder floating around in the air and those hardly tolerable floral perfumes—torn between the urge to flee right then and there and the compulsion to pester the young woman with all sorts of requests so the session would last and last. The trams kept trundling by and the streetlamps were already turning on, and she was applying foundation for this and foundation for that, then this powder, then that powder, then a lip pencil and an eye pencil, then two kinds of lipstick, then three shades of rouge, then five shades of eye shadow, then who knows how many layers of mascara. But when she brought me the hand mirror to have a look, the process all seemed too quick. The final result did astonish me. I didn't look like myself at all. It's not that I looked bad, but under such thick makeup I could see too little of myself to be able to judge whether or not I was beautiful. Unsure, I got down from the seat and took a few tentative steps around the room while my head was spinning, and only then did I remember to buy something to compensate for the makeover. After brief consideration, I settled on red lipstick and nail polish in the same shade. When I went out into the street, I was at a loss for a full half minute about where to take myself next. No matter which direction I looked in, there were too many eyes, ears, and noses. The tap of thousands of high heels, the rustle of shirts, the restless shimmy of dresses. Hubbub interrupted by the squeal of trams. Laughter. Beggars without legs. A woman begging with children. Glowing phones. Shouts. The aroma of pizza. Well-lit merchandise in the windows, which in the early dark acquired an air of sanctity. I set out and headed south, but people were walking toward me; they kept walking toward me. Hladna, if only you'd seen those faces. The hairdos and eyeglasses in different-colored plastic. The way they kept their hands in their pockets. None of them had ever done anything bad. I heard a siren, far away at first, but no matter how much I turned this way or that way to evade it, I kept miscalculating and the sound only grew louder. It might have been from a fire brigade, or the police, or even an ambulance—I've never been good at telling the distinguishing between different sirens. It must have passed by quite close, because at one point the sound became alarmingly loud, yet I saw nothing. Then the siren's wail faded, as if it were on its way to Medveščak. I didn't dare turn to see whether there was smoke billowing above the roofs. Instead, I walked and walked. Only when I happened upon a small restaurant where, in my past life, I'd sometimes dined with Igor did I feel as if I'd arrived at a destination. I entered without a second thought. This was a good place to hide, because most of the dining area wasn't visible from the street. Although it was dinnertime, there weren't many guests. A family of three; a middle-aged man who looked as if he were waiting for someone; two young men. I was seated at a small table in the corner, at the very back, where I could watch everything that was happening yet still preserve my feeling of being out of sight. The waiter, a boy so young and thin that his white shirt and bow tie seemed unconvincing, appeared at the table before I had a chance to look at the menu, so in my desire to avoid attracting attention, I gave him the same order Igor and I had enjoyed before: sardines, Swiss chard, and white wine, with fish pâté for the appetizer. This was one of those restaurants that go for the warm, homey atmosphere. Red-brick walls, simple upholstered chairs, bulky wooden tables. Tile stoves in the corners and antique irons on the shelves. The music was playing so softly, you couldn't place the genre. I leaned against the wall, exhausted. My cheeks were blazing and my body shook with an agreeable tremor, something like relief. But the problem, Hladna, was that in places like this, and elsewhere, a person mustn't be alone for too long. Whoever is too alone begins to feel the inner fragility of things. The trickiness of impressions. The artificiality of the atmosphere. The fact that someone had spent a whole day at the Hrelić flea market to find an antique iron for the shelf. In this corner we'll build a tile stove, said the then proprietor, people will feel at home here and order more meat dishes, better wine, they won't be able to resist the dessert. Everything was a performance with lousy stage sets. The middle-aged man by the window who wore his glasses halfway down his nose and had spread open his newspaper—was he waiting for someone to join him? Or had he assumed this silly, old-fashioned pose for some other reason? The young men sitting by the entrance whispered the whole time as they showed each other things on their phones. Both had bangs, so with each move they had to brush the hair away from their eyes and kept flicking their heads. Was one of them glancing my way? And as for the family in the middle of the room—how did the kid in the *Star Wars* tracksuit fit in with the grown-ups she was sitting with, who were dressed for work? At least I could have been given a more convincing waiter, I thought, watching the skinny kid who was racing around as if the dining room were overflowing, while his clothing, older and slower than he was, stuck to his body, and though he did glance over at me from time to time, as if surprised that I was still here, he did not bring me my food. Only when I became aware of the wife in the family of three *really* looking over at me did I collect my thoughts. Or, more precisely: I traded one form of dread for another, this one far more real. In her haphazard, poorly concealed scrutiny there was a sense that she knew who I was, and I was finally forced to take a closer look at her. She had a familiar, pointy face, a little like one of those African wooden figures with the jutting, almond-shaped eyes. It was Marta, a girl I'd known when we were students. I tried pretending I didn't know her, but she had already spotted my recognition of her, and though she kept refraining from looking over, the change in her demeanor was perfectly obvious. Her husband noticed this too. He asked her something, looked repeatedly in my direction, exchanged a few more words with her, got up, and, to my horrified surprise, came over and said, "My wife is uncomfortable about this, but she knows you and would like to say hello." He had a foreign accent, which gave what he said an amusing pomposity. I looked over at Marta and smiled, and she, red with embarrassment, responded with a smile and a quick little wave. "If you're not joining anyone else for dinner, would you do us the honor of coming to our table? We would be so glad," he said. His eyes circled around the ceiling as if there were words up there he was choosing carefully before inserting them into his sentences, and this lent a wry overtone to what he was saying. He seemed kind; his accent gave him an air of sweetness, but in his manner there was something police-like, and I didn't know how to counter it. "No, no," I stammered, "I wouldn't want to impose." But I was already speaking while burdened by a secret, and my voice was not able to muster a resolute refusal. And Marta was of no help; her awkward plea that he should leave me alone was also faltering. So, after a few more moments of pointless back-and-forth, I picked up my purse and took the seat next to Marta's husband, across from a dark-haired little five- or six-year-old girl, apparently their daughter. I had the feeling that the child's outfit had been a bone of contention earlier that evening, but I couldn't quite put my finger on which position each of them had taken in the dispute. "My tooth fell out," said the little girl, grinning. I didn't know what to say, so I said nothing. "Now they've moved me into the lion cub group at day care, which is way better than the little butterflies," she said. I had nothing to add. "Don't pester Auntie," said Marta wearily. She'd been the one critical of the tracksuit. Only then did I notice how much she'd changed. She'd lost her former glow that, despite the unusual features of her face, or perhaps precisely because of them, had given her remarkable beauty. Her figure hadn't changed; she was still slender, and she combed her long blonde hair the same way, but now she seemed all beige. Behind her narrow prescription glasses, her gaze was pointier still, and her pale-blue irises had acquired an inorganic fragility, a little like decorative pieces of glass. She seemed more vulnerable now. Her husband, Nihat, a burly, dark-haired man from Turkey, showed such respect for me from the start, with such sincerity, that I accepted him with a measure of caution. He seemed to have wrongly assumed that Marta and I had been close friends. From the start, she, on the other hand, was embarrassed by my presence, as if I knew something about her that I shouldn't know, or she knew something about me. In a panic, I combed through my memories, but I couldn't pin down anything that might be the source of her embarrassment. We were merely classmates, never close friends. I may have found her a little off-putting, a woman who used her beauty as a defense mechanism. I may have been slightly envious, but I couldn't remember ever clashing with her, or going through anything crucial together. Only when Nihat said, "I'm very glad to meet a colleague of Marta's who has been so successful," and she shot him a sideways glance, did I cotton on to the source of the embarrassment. People often think of themselves, isn't that right, Hladna? They think they're unsuccessful because they work in the municipal bureaucracy, while across the table from them is a peer who has been lauded with awards for her designs. They might be done up in full makeup, elegant, but still they are swamped by anxiety. They don't notice that this person from their past's eyes have an odd glow; the fingers she's using to pick through her sardines are swollen and shaky. They don't really see each other. Just then I felt grateful for their blindness. I relaxed. A surge of generous mercy swept me toward these people. "Yes," I said, "awards are lovely, but there are months of hard work behind them." "Yes," I said, "it is great to work in the studio of a legendary architect like Elena Sajko, but Igor and I, in fact, do most of the work. All Elena contributes is her name." "Yes," I said, "when you're handed your doctoral degree, you realize it's only the beginning." "Yes," I said, "all the travel is wearing." I even went so far as to call the waiter over and order a bottle of wine for the table. I wore them down with my charm.

He went quiet and slumped into his chair, undoing two buttons on his shirt and fingering the hairs on his chest, while a mild serenity came over her as she followed my every move with her smile. Only the little girl sat up straight and watched me with a distrustful, slanting gaze. "My mama's an architect," she said. "Please be quiet," said Marta nervously, "and finish your food." When her husband took out his phone and began fiddling with it, she leaned over the table to me, and her voice took on a certain intimacy. "How did you and Igor begin collaborating?" she asked. "When we were students, I never saw the two of you together." You'd be surprised, Hladna, but, seriously, at that very moment, I thought of Igor's jaw, of his surprisingly tender, porcelain cheeks that I caught sight of for the first time when he shaved three years earlier, right before his wedding. The image of his smooth jaw filled me with an amorphous dread. "Weeell," I stammered, "he was working with Elena, practically running the show there, while I was working with the Old Man—better if I don't use his name, he builds these antediluvian houses—and then I defended my doctorate, and then without the Old Man knowing it I submitted a proposal for a fish-processing plant, won the competition, and was given an award. Then Igor heard of me and called me, and I went over to them." I stopped talking all of a sudden, so abruptly that the conversation suddenly sank away. We all sat there slumped in our silence, even the little girl. "Look at this," said Nihat, staring at his phone. "This evening there were fires in three Zagreb apartments in three different places. I hope ours isn't one of them." He chuckled. "Marta, did you snuff out the incense sticks?" She glared at him with scorn. I felt as if a fire were burning right there in my chest and traveling to my ears. I quickly signaled the waiter and offered to pay. They protested politely. As I was folding my wallet, it hit me: the hundred and ten kunas in there was all the money I had left. We walked out of the restaurant together. While we were standing there on the sidewalk, awkwardly saying our goodbyes, the little girl suddenly hugged me, and then leaped back to her mother and shyly pressed against her side. Both parents laughed and stroked her head. This gesture, this tender simultaneous acceptance, reminded me that the evening was cold. I shivered. I was tempted to ask them to put me up, but such a thing would have been impossible to say. They had parked in front of the restaurant, and after I watched them get into their car and drive off, a weakness came over me.

Where to now? The fact that I had nowhere to go back to was suddenly very real. The city had emptied, stores were closing, and the lights left on in the vacant buildings really turned them into something like a sanctuary. The mannequins in the shop display acquired the serene indifference of sacred statuary. There was nobody who could help me. I don't know why I then headed back toward the main square. Maybe subconsciously I felt a need to be nearer to Medveščak, to sniff the air, to see whether the passersby were looking at me with more friendly eyes. I headed northeast, but, again for no real reason, I went toward Vlaška Street. I am telling you, I had no particular plan in mind; I didn't have it in me to plan. I just walked and walked and walked, and walked straight into a store simply because it was open. A solution of sorts. Only when I was inside did I see that the store was selling an array of cordage. Red, yellow, blue, thick as a python, skinny as spaghetti, coarse and smooth, white ropes and ordinary brownish ropes. At first it seemed as if there was nobody there—at least no humans—just wheels of rope with the authority of creatures that had chosen silence. The wine I'd had with dinner took hold and I was already seriously considering plunking myself down on the floor, with a powerful urge to curl up in a fetal position, when I was stopped by the sudden arrival of the shopkeeper, who jumped out from the back room a mite too vigorously, as if he'd been doing something he wasn't supposed to be doing. "May I help you?" he asked. This threw me off. He wanted to help me? Where to start, good man, railed my weary inner self, should I tell you the story of my whole life, or do I limit it to just this afternoon? Might I ask you whether I may sleep here among the ropes? Perhaps such a thing wouldn't be out of the question.

BEDBUGS 39

He seemed like a harmless enough young man, a good soul, with slightly protruding ears and a calflike gaze. But then he began asking ticklish questions. People tend to do this, don't they? People ask: Why sleep in my shop? Who are you? Where are you from? What are you running from? Have you set somebody's apartment on fire? People are bored, so these things interest them. After eyeing the coils of rope, I uttered, "How much does this rope cost?" "Which one?" he answered affably. But something about the way he briefly stopped and grew serious before he started speaking, while the protruding tips of his ears went all red, made the question difficult. Yes, we both know which rope I'd buy, and what I'd be using it for. I looked him straight in the eyes, which, as with sloths, peeked dreamily from under his half-closed lids, but I didn't see anything there. Ruddy cheeks and a smooth child's chin gave him a doltish look that held no evil. Yet his question remained hanging in the air for a little too long, waiting patiently the way a noose awaits its neck. I know what you'll say, but don't judge me, Hladna. There was no other way out, can you see that? If a person is to accept and bear their punishment, they should know whether or not they're guilty. There was nothing inside me, no guilt or innocence, just a vast loneliness sitting in my lungs or my throat, or on my brain, or in the headlights of the cars that watched me as if I were on a crosswalk, or in the windows that gave no thought to opening, or in the shopkeeper's question that didn't care what I'd do with the rope he sold me. "I need ordinary white rope, as sturdy as possible, weight-bearing, and easy to tie in a knot," I said coldly. He said not a word. Stepping behind the counter, he took hold of one of the coils. "This one?" "Yes, that one." "Thirty kunas." "Per meter?" "Yes." I stroked the ribbed rope like the spine of an obedient dog, thinking about how many meters I'd need. Two would be too little. If I took three, I'd be spending nearly all the money I had left, and the decision would be final. I didn't have enough for four, and four might be what I'd need. There can be no failed attempts, so the rope might have to be wrapped around something several times. Around what? I imagined myself leaving the cordage shop and looking for what to hang myself from. There were trees everywhere, but the branches could snap easily. The seat on a child's swing is more reliable, but too low to the ground. How to find a peaceful spot where a late-night stroller won't bother me with stories about the wonders of life? And where to find a chair? Cities are not well suited to a hanging. People die more decently here, in beds from overdoses and in bathtubs full of bloody water, while public parks and children's playgrounds are not defiled; if one is throwing oneself off of high-rises or under trains, this generally happens on the outskirts of town, where the transparency of the space quickly obscures every act. For a hanging to be convincing, what you really need is a barn, a cow munching on its cud casually next to the swinging body, and the creaking of the beam like a soft song of consolation for those who are left behind. This was an easy way to contemplate suicide, because it was still only a possibility. A person always imagines their own death in the eyes of others, right? To look into the void with one's own eyes is only possible for someone who no longer feels as if anything from life belongs to them. And I still had my hundred ten kunas, so when the shopkeeper measured out three meters, snipped his scissors, and asked, "Should I?" I went silent. The coiled rope was only rope, and it had the potential to become anything, but a three-meter length, cut to order, becomes a hanging rope. I can't remember whether I mumbled something, I can't remember whether I said anything more to the shopkeeper; all I remember is that I turned, left the store, and began walking east along Vlaška Street. The clock at Kvaternik Square gave the time as 9:15, dew had already condensed on the parked cars and the street, and more and more windows were lighting up on the dark facades. People were retreating into their homes. I crossed my arms and held tight, shivering in my thin cotton dress. I tried looking at the shop windows, imagining the cozy interiors of the stores, but my gaze kept being drawn to the blinking of a traffic light in the distance. Green. Yellow. Red. Time was passing, the fire had surely gained in ferocity, and the street stretched before me as the only possible path out of the city. Be quick, be quick, I whispered and strode on and on. But at the intersection of Maksimirska and Bukovačka Streets, I could go no farther. Across the pedestrian crosswalk lay Maksimir Park, dark Maksimir with its hundred-year-old trees, sturdy swing seats, and deep lakes. Maksimir, beyond which lay nothing but a long stretch of road leading off to the Pannonian barrens. I stood there for a few moments, hesitating, then turned right. Here, like always, I was soon disappointed. The postapocalyptic area in front of the Zagreb University Faculty of Economics and Business; the god-awful edifice of the private university that stood next to it. The pseudo-Chicago atmosphere that always drove me to laughter interlaced with nausea. The skyscraper with its many eyes was on guard to the east; the only direction I could go was westward, back toward the city center. I tried to see the road, the cars, the occasional trams, the predictable roots of the trees along the tree-lined avenue, but bearing down on my left temple I felt only the heavy darkness within, crowded by all of these buildings, examples of bad historicism or solid neo-styles marred by the later addition of a railing, a window, overhanging eaves, a tacky sign, a flowerpot of the wrong color. A familiar malaise overcame me: Is there nobody in this country who loves architecture enough to at least shut up if they have nothing good or essential to say? Maybe my anger saved me. With it I could think again as an architect and not as a woman who was on the run because she'd set someone's apartment on fire. If it hadn't been for the bad architecture and that statue by the post office of a naked woman being sprayed by water—as if urine or sperm—I would have had to be aware that the time was nearly 10 p.m., and it was surely too late, and from now on I would have to stay well away from the police. As it was, I simply walked, already used to the cold, and the city densified and grew, and ugly buildings elbowed their way in among the more attractive ones. At the roundabout where the street ended, there it was, waiting solemnly, well lit and white, my prize after the long trek—as you may already have guessed—the Meštrović Pavilion. There is finer architecture, finer indeed, in the city of Zagreb, but no building commands its site with greater grace, reining in even the most aggressive neoclassical building around it. When a person sits down on any of its steps, between any two of its columns, as I did just then, they'll think they're better than the life they've been living. Behind my back, and beyond the pavilion, the city center was or wasn't, burning or not burning, while the streets ahead of me ran off for a long way in many directions. Another person or car would pass, the trams squealed wearily, earthy smells wafted from the grass, but otherwise the night was still. I perched on my purse, hugged my knees, leaned on the inner face of a column, and tried to sleep. I don't know when it was that I noticed the teenagers. They were on the other side of the building, but their voices circled around the rotunda inside the colonnade, echoing off the stone walls and the glass on the windows, ringing and groaning and trumpeting right in my ears. There might have been six or seven of them: by their voices I could only count two girls and three boys, but there are always the silent ones who want to be accepted by groups like these. If you'd only heard them, Hladna. How affected their laughter was. They chewed their cookies and nibbled their potato chips with their quick teeth, nervously ripped the wrappers off chocolate candies, burped and then laughed again, rolled empty glass bottles around on the rough stone floor, used words like "bro" and "random," gave off sharp, incoherent shrieks, and then there was an even more sudden, irritating quiet. Animals. Did they have to remind me so noisily that there was something beyond the pavilion? That Medveščak was near and the night was awaiting my final decision? Will I really flee? I knew the die had been cast. Prince Višeslav Street was stretching out there before me, running straight to the intercity bus terminal, but my thinking had been that my next move might be postponed a little bit longer—I could catch up on sleep, and the morning might bring a fresh frame of mind. All this had its appeal. Now, however, the next move could no longer be put off. I had to get away, I thought, from the teenagers' voices that were bludgeoning me. As far away as I could get, on the first bus out. I reached the terminal at 10:46 p.m. and immediately purchased a ticket. The last bus for my hometown was leaving at 11. A night bus. Is there anything worse? When the lights are turned off and you struggle in vain to fall asleep amid the musty smells of other people's feet. But at that very moment there was no better place for me. It felt so good to be in the warmth, on a soft, comfortable seat, putting my feet up on the footrest, stretching out, leaning my head back, putting down my bag and dozing in the stuffy darkness where only the occasional phone, ineffectively aggressive, smoldered like a giant firefly and broadcast a television series, movie, or music, a rerun, something soothingly humdrum. There was only a handful of travelers, no more than a dozen, so the voices of the two drivers, who maintained a constant stream of conversation to keep themselves awake, were easy to hear. I sat on one of the front seats and felt as if the driver were speaking to me directly. "Wow, the trouble I got up to during Yugo times"—I found his bourbony voice soothing—"I was the wildest madman you can imagine. There was once a time, believe it or not, when I drove all the way to Sremska Mitrovica in a truck that was supposed to be delivering merchandise to Banja Luka from Zenica. It was all about a woman, if you get my drift. She had these big tits, and boy oh boy could she spin a tale. But then the truck broke down somewhere near Bijeljina. I took off and left the woman and the truck, and like a shot I hopped on a bus for Sarajevo, then to Split, then straight to the beach to hustle those German babes. Later they came after me, believe you me. And when I was in the army, what I got away with, better you don't know. I told this one major he should wash because he smelled so foul. See? Can you imagine how green he turned? But I did my time, God knows. Two weeks of solitary, have you any idea?" On and on like that. From the 1970s to now, from the Vardar in Macedonia to Mount Triglav in Slovenia, from Vienna to Oslo, from the United States to Japan. Arsonists of the world unite. There are those of us who cannot comprehend ourselves, but we do know about demolition. Architecture longs to rid itself of what has been foisted on it. I couldn't see either of the drivers, but I imagined the one who was driving to be scrawny, mildly hunched over, in his early sixties, with long, dangling arms and a cigarette wedged between his fingers like a sixth burning digit, a tall fellow, rumpled, dark-haired, with gray eyes and dark circles beneath them, his cheeks creased, no lips, wrung dry to the last drop by life, to absolute solidity. This is the only way to travel to your hometown without fear. To lean your head on the window and watch how the shoulder of the highway courses by monotonously, without a single thought for reading the traffic signs, billboards, and other markers. After almost two hours on the road, we stopped at a gas station. Just in time for my bladder, where the wine from the restaurant was now tensely waiting. The night was cool but pleasant, and there was nobody in the restroom. The soothing smell of the disinfectant, the pure white light. While I was peeing in a half crouch, I had a look at my panties. I have never gone to bed wearing dirty underwear; this is a rule I've always observed, both before and after the car crash. Habits can be dangerous, but they are necessary for survival. And you, you'd be lost without your afternoon pelin bitters, wouldn't you? So how can you not understand that right then and there, I stripped off my panties and tossed them into the wastebasket next to the toilet, and then pulled the black panties with the white hearts from my purse—the ones I'd salvaged at the last minute from the apartment—and put them on. Doing this filled me with an eerie chill. Hadn't I stripped off panties, black ones with black lace edging, in this very same restroom on an unusually warm early morning in February? I could hear the feeble buzz of the highway, the trucks having trouble starting up, somebody noisily bursting into the next stall and peeing even more noisily. Where was Sergej? Was he waiting for me in the car or smoking by the door? I remember the smell of coffee hitting me as I came out; I remember that soon after this, Sergej turned off the highway onto an old road. Why? Yes, I was the one who asked him to, but I don't know why. I remember that while we were driving along the old road, I opened a bag of mixed nuts. Now I shut my eyes to peer again into the silvery depths of that bag, facing the disarray of walnuts, hazelnuts, almonds, pistachios, peanuts, cashews, and Brazil nuts. No order, no principle, just the bewilderment of a burgeoning spring. I remember thinking: this tastes awful. Did I offer some to Sergej? I don't know. Panties, snacks, the dark, the hospital, that's all I can summon. I stood before the big mirror in the same bathroom now, warming my hands under a stream of hot water and having a look at myself. What was this broad, dark, angular country face hiding? The prominent cheekbones, now even more striking with the rouge, gave me an expression of constant wry amusement, as if in the dimples to the right and left of my mouth I were hiding something I was slyly refusing to say. Father's stubborn straight eyebrows and the curly hair that had come down on Mother's side to my sister Anica and her children, to my sister Irma, to Maria's Rina, but never eluded control as much as it did in my case, frizzy and riotous, to the point that the only way for me to rein it in was to iron it daily. Now, the blonde dye had long since washed out, and the brown woolly curls lent my face something gutsy, down-to-earth, pragmatic. I wasn't as skinny as usual, and in the close-fitting black dress with classical lines, I no longer looked svelte, but sturdy, like a middle-aged laborer, with big breasts, muscular arms, and big hips. Full lips still could, indeed, transform a face; when I smiled softly, my dark eyes acquired a friendly, lively warmth. But when I gave a big smile, there were my uneven teeth, the underbite and jutting cuspids, and my face crossed over, becoming something that eluded simple definition. There was a trace there from childhood, something irregular and contained, something that tended to free itself and improve, but also something later, here, in the little birdlike nose, something that was only out to demolish, without any real notion of the possibilities of building anew. Uncomfortably emphasized by the already congealing makeup, my face told me I shouldn't be here, in this bathroom—against the white background of the walls and tiles, I was unneedfully asserting myself; I had made a really big mistake. Looking at my face was unbearable, so I looked at my hands under the stream of water and felt how its warmth was spreading through my body and relaxing it. Only then did a deep, raspy voice, thundering suddenly behind me, declare, "Come on, girlie, we're waiting for you!" and summon me back to reality. It was the bus driver who had been entertaining and consoling me all evening with his sins from the past. He wasn't at all like what I'd imagined.

He had meaty lips and hungry, lazy eyes, with long hair uncombed on the nape of his neck, and while I followed him to the bus, his broad hips—which wobbled on his bones like a sack of sand over knock knees—filled me with a feeling of something ponderous. Awaiting me were my hometown and my family, large and incomprehensible. We drove another hour before we left the highway. The clock on the bus gave the time as 2:31 a.m. when the first houses began to appear on the outskirts. Everything was like it had been two years before, but with more lights. How to describe this architecture of taverns, grill joints, and car washes? The white pillars standing there on the balconies, self-satisfied, like bared teeth, the clash of neon signs, the houses occupying space as if there were no other houses around them, the facades whose colors pierced the eye even in the dark, the gardens with statues of the Virgin Mary and concrete lions on the garden posts, and the chickens roasting 24/7 on open spits. Constant idiotic violence perpetrated against the landscape. Yet this tormented ambience received me with a kind of grace. The shrubs and tree-lined avenues were serene and massive as if this were midsummer, and when we got off at the pleasantly lit bus terminal, I was surprised by the warmth of the night into which I could dive quite naturally, as if into a friendly hug. The sleepy taxi drivers who offered their services purely for the sake of decorum, the ramshackle tables and chairs in the bus terminal's café in a blessed tranquility. The asphalt, oily from the lights, almost soft. The welcoming entrances to the pinball clubs and gambling halls. While I was walking toward the center, I listened to my own footsteps as if listening to the ticking of a clock in a dark room: with an altogether mellow, almost cozy, dread. In the parking lots the cars were sleeping, the carts out in front of the shopping center were sleeping, the local people were sleeping, the firefighters were sleeping, the police were sleeping, my sister Anica and her family—my family—were sleeping in their house in the center of town. The night was in the phase when it gave the impression of being infinite, and my hometown still wasn't demanding anything of me—it was just quietly offering up its familiar places. I walked by the high school in the park. Shining warmly in the dark were the wooden benches where Ante and I had idled away countless hours. I've mentioned Ante to you, haven't I? Anica's youngest son, my nephew, my stand-in for a brother, my classmate. Now, his dear face appeared so alive in my mind that I probably smiled. His mild, watery eyes, quite crossed behind his glasses; his crooked, broad lips that cracked into a smile like a clothesline, with his sharp teeth hanging out to dry; his big ears; his tousled hair, planted on his scalp like a nest; his chin with the here-and-there whiskers. A face on which the features seemed slapped together at random, at the last moment, always on the run toward their source, yet nothing could be corrected on it without destroying the viability of the whole. We sat on those benches after morning classes were over, or during long summer afternoons when the house was too crowded, or on cool Saturday nights. He smoked and I drank wine. We talked about boys, less often about school and friends, seldom about family, but most of all about the buildings we hoped to make. He planned to furnish them and I planned their design. Sometimes we said nothing at all. He had the rare gift of keeping quiet in an easygoing way, but when he was smoking at the time, with that soft style of his, he seemed older and wiser than usual, and I'd lean on his shoulder and hug his free arm like a warm pillow, and I wouldn't be able to fend off optimism. The park and my hometown were confining and boring, surrounding us, here as they always had and would, but in those moments we felt something different was in store. If I could have called him just then, I thought as I passed by a little cove where the boats were creaking sleepily, would he admit to remembering how we rowed out to sea one night in a dinghy we'd stolen? How old could we have been? Sixteen? Seventeen? We had a third with us, a boy Ante liked at the time, a kid who had just moved here from inland and was still in awe of everything about the sea. Ante rowed; I navigated from the bow. The oars seemed too long and kept knocking other boats, wood hitting wood like metal hitting metal. It felt like a whole eternity before we pulled free of the harbor, but the boats and the town that loomed behind them slipping away from us as if Ante were pushing them away with his arms— that made me love my nephew-brother forever, above and beyond any merit. The season may have been early spring; the night was downright cold. When we were out near the middle of the canal, the wind picked up. "That's to be expected," said Ante over his shoulder to the boy who was huddling in the stern. I tried to catch Ante's eye, but there was nothing for me to see but the big hulk of his body, rowing with more vigor than was in his nature. Why such a dark night? Maybe the clouds had already blanketed the sky by then, and not later, once we'd ventured farther from town, navigating in among the islands, when we realized we wouldn't be able to avoid a squall. The sea had tricked us, as it had tricked so many before us. I reckon you've never been out to sea when a storm is rising. I'll tell you, Hladna: the illusion then is that you're not there with anybody else. All you know is the drenching darkness, the clench in your throat, the freezing eyeballs, the cold penetrating to the warmest parts of your belly and rocking you the way a kid tips a bug in his hand before he squashes it. I patted the inside of the boat, but nothing could offer a secure outcome. I smelled Ante's sweat and clearly imagined how he was feeling both terribly cold and terribly hot, how red splotches were rising on his thick neck, how a prickling panic was running down his back, because he wasn't certain anymore of having a grip on both oars. "Maybe we should call for help," I heard him mutter through the wind and rain, helplessly clutching his arms to his belly. "We will not!" I yelled sharply. No surprise there, Hladna. Ante was Anica and Dragan's child, but I was a sister to four grown-ups, and I always felt as if I ought to be older than I was. That I shouldn't have to steal rowboats. Was I really prepared to place my own life and the lives of others in jeopardy out of sheer vanity? Oh, yes, I was. Something inside me spurred me to tackle the most challenging of math problems, to design brilliant buildings—the tenacity of a child who was a grown-up even before she was born, who always had to prove to everyone she could manage on her own. I turned around in the dark; some of the lights I could see must be reachable. If only you knew how joyfully scampish I was when I saw that one of the smaller islands was quite close by, but that we had better chances of landing not there but on the southern shores of two larger ones. These two numbskulls, I thought, would rather call on their mommies to save them. I told the boy in the stern to paddle with his hands on the port side while I paddled on the starboard. The waves were so big that my winter jacket was soaked to the shoulders, my face was sprayed on all sides, and my wet hair was plastered to my cheeks, but I felt no chill at all. The cold came later, once we'd landed. A few fishermen helped us tie up at the wharf, and from somewhere they produced dry blankets. Once we were on land, the storm didn't seem so dreadful. It was an ordinary light downpour with a little wind, but I couldn't stop shivering. I remember we went somewhere briefly to warm up, to a cellar or the home of one of the fishermen, and that same night we rowed back the same way we'd come. The boy in the stern was excited beyond all measure by the events and could not stop talking. I watched his teeth gleaming in the moonlight, his stupid apelike arms gesticulating, so I told Ante, "Hey there, birdie boy, you may wear a Che Guevara T-shirt, but rowing is definitely not your forte." Can you believe such a sentence ever crossed my lips? This made him angry, and he gave me the oars. Later the story made the rounds for a time among kids our age, but somehow it didn't reach Anica and Dragan. I was so scared the word might get out that I softened my arrogance. I stopped claiming to be smarter than everybody else and badgering my teachers. Maybe that rowboat is why I was later able to defend my doctoral thesis. But why think about this now? Now, when my doctoral thesis wasn't going to be of any help, when I was bereft of all vanity and was nodding off, if briefly, on a bench in a park, on an unpeopled waterfront. Every recollection of emotion is painful in its own way, wouldn't you say, Hladna? And yet my rising pain felt good. I enjoyed becoming a person again. My family was really there, nearby; I felt how they were wetly smacking their lips in their sleep, farting and snoring. Soon they'd wake up, and they'd love me or they wouldn't, they'd think of me or they wouldn't, they'd expect me or they wouldn't. A coolness set in before dawn. I straightened up, lifted my feet to the bench, and hugged my knees. Before first light, people began passing by, walking their dogs. A short woman with a small, slow dog, a hunched man and a small, quick dog. The shifting of gravel under their steps, the odor of urine, their dark figures silvered by the predawn moonlight. I watched them, hidden in the shadows of the trees. Then two men arrived with fishing rods. They sat quite far apart but from time to time tossed brief sentences, raw phrases, back and forth, and these seemed to slice off pieces of the darkness and hasten daybreak. I covered my ears with my hands, tucked my head between my knees, and closed my eyes. Soon. Soon the night will drop away and everybody will be able to see me. Behind my eyelids, on the inside of my mouth, the darkness there felt familiar and warm, but the fresh smells of the new day kept breaking through to my nose. The smell of the fish splashing in the buckets of the two fishermen, the fragrance of the flowers under the trees, the smell of the gravel damp with morning dew. Bread, rosemary, coffee, combusting gasoline. I could feel someone slow, perhaps an early-morning housekeeper, walking right past me. Then someone heavy-footed and hurrying. I opened my eyes and ears. The day had almost fully dawned, and everything was recognizing me in a parental sort of way, both intimate and cool. All the benches knew I had deliberately pushed away my first real boyfriend, because I was afraid that with him, I'd never get away from this town. The sea knew I didn't like going alone to visit Mother on the island, because she and I never had anything to talk about. The closest café knew I didn't like drinking hard liquor, because I couldn't bear the loss of control. The surrounding buildings knew I loved them. It seemed as if any minute now somebody might come, point a finger at me, and shout, "That's her! The one who set fire to the apartment in Zagreb and ran away!" I slipped off my shoes and cautiously stood. Every bone and muscle in my body ached, and I had an irresistible urge to do a little yoga, or at least have a good quick stretch, but I resisted. Please, no unnecessary movements. Here, right behind my back, across the road and three blocks farther on, was the police station. And closer still, across the road and only one block away, on the corner, stood Anica and Dragan's house. I rummaged for my mirror, a tissue, and rouge from my purse, fixed what could be fixed, tidied my hair as much as I was able, smoothed my dress with my hands, and set off in that direction. Like each morning for the last twenty-five and more years, there was Dragan sitting on the doorstep, drinking coffee and smoking. "Hey," he said, expressionless, as if he'd been seeing me every day. "Hey," I said. My own voice, deep and hoarse, sounded out of place on the narrow stone-paved street, empty and still slippery from the morning dew, so all I did was stand there, leaning on the little table where Dragan's coffee was steaming. I said nothing. I was waiting for him to speak first. It didn't take long for me to remember: he had always looked this way, as if he had something to say, but actually what he'd say was more or less the same as what he was thinking. "How goes it?" I asked. "Retired," he said. And smiled. I noticed he really had aged. While his expression was solemn, serious, the central point of his face was his bushy yellowish mustache, from which his cigarette smoke billowed as if the whiskers were quickly expanding then shrinking—a playful and wise mustache under his crooked nose, the mustache of a man who had waltzed into town in the late 1970s, a rake, after ten years on a ship; he had been everywhere and seen everything, a man who had, by now, been married forever to my good sister. But when he smiled, his false teeth took center stage, and, oversized and alien, they made more visible the aging of his face, his whole body, his sagging cheeks, the dark bags under his motionless little eyes, the deformity of his earlobes, the scrawniness of his arms, the jaundiced tinge of his skin. The body of a man who had been waiting twenty-five years for the reopening of the textile factory where he used to maintain the equipment. "Your mother's inside," he said, as if I had asked about Mother. The small window on the front door, the yellowing lace curtain that had been there for so long nobody dared touch it, watched me and waited. Cautiously I pressed the latch. The familiar squeal of the hinges, the deep disgruntlement of the wood. As soon as I descended the two steps into the kitchen, I felt the cold of the tiles I knew so well under the soles of my shoes, creaking as if my footsteps were hurting them, as if, faced with each exaggeration, with happiness or anger, they might easily fracture and fling each of us into the deep sea hidden below. I needed a little time for my eyes to acclimate to the gloom that was always there on the ground floor; between the small window above the kitchen sink and the sun there stood the wall of a neighbor's house. The table was in its old place, in the middle of the room, a new pellet stove by the wall to its right, and next to it, where the old cast-iron stove used to stand, there were new shelves full of spices, grains, and legumes such as I'd never seen in this house. The sink and cookstove with a little stretch of countertop between were still standing along the outside wall. Straight ahead, the hallway with the bathroom door on the right. Beyond the corner of the bathroom, an exit into a miniature indoor garden and the beginning of the stairs that wound around the bedrooms on the first and second floors. Only when I turned to look at the china closet standing against the partition wall of the bathroom, stuffed with mementos from various weddings, floral porcelain cups, the occasional crucifix, crystalware that was never used, lace and ugly souvenirs from high school excursions, did I notice Mother. She wasn't moving, but as soon as I sank my gaze into the heap of kitschy junk, both predictable and eluding description, I knew she was there. She was lying in the corner between the china closet and the walls, on an ancient moss-green trunk, which, with the help of a mattress, had been transformed into a hospital bed. To be honest, Hladna, I was shocked. "Milka, Milka," I murmured, not without reproach. I may have also said this loudly. I don't know if you'll understand me; it's not as if Milka had ever been particularly lively or had ambitions that she'd never die. But to find her there on that trunk, skin and bones, stiff as a board, her mouth loose, toothless, drooling, letting her hair stick to her forehead, her deteriorating body stinking up her son-in-law's kitchen—this I couldn't believe. My mother, who'd always perceived me as a blunder that should never have happened, disgraceful proof of late-in-life passion, a woman who, after our father died, no longer knew what lunch and dinner were for, how to launder clothes, how to work in the fields, prune olive trees, or clean fish, for whom somebody always had to play the father, whether it was Anica, Dragan, or even the grandchildren, who never raised her voice, who knew how to bake cakes only when asked. How dare she lie there dying so frankly, so brazenly? I sat on a chair that was right next to the head of the trunk-bed. Her eyes were closed, but the way she was breathing showed she wasn't asleep. What could I say? My whole life she'd been at a loss for what to do with me. I wasn't her grandchild and she couldn't believe I was her daughter, so we used go-betweens to converse: first Father, and later my sisters, brother, nephew, or one of the locals. With time we developed a "language" all our own. In her presence I'd say to Anica, or Maria, or Ante, "Looks to me like Milka's fixing to get married, have a look at the sweater she's wearing," and she'd say to Anica, Maria, Ante, or whoever else happened to be in the room at the time, "Nobody loves a person who talks too much." And then all of us would have a laugh. But when the two of us were left alone, both of us would go crazy. What could I say to her? I turned the armchair toward the wall, leaned over on the armrest, and inspected her arm. Despite her lack of exposure to the sun, she was tanned and her arms still had the appealing warmth I'd loved. Sometimes, when a late island evening found me at her kitchen table in front of the television set, which both of us conversed with, I'd reach over and say, "Warm up my hand!" Milka would rub it, tenderly and vigorously, as if she were bringing a being to life from mud. Now I reached for her hands, wanting to stroke them, but I was shattered when I discovered they were uncomfortably clammy. She was wearing her wedding ring and the almond shape of her fingernails, the only thing she'd inherited from her large family, was still recognizable, but aside from that there was nothing left on Milka's trunk-bed—not her big eyes with the long lashes, always a little sparse, nor the full lips forever pursed in something like a question that hadn't yet been asked, nor the red in her cheeks, the consequence of the permanent shame of a teenage girl from the mainland marrying an only child from the islands. There was nothing left of all of that, only a body producing shit and piss and gas and drool and sweat, guided by the cruel automatism of nature. And the smell, Hladna. Like chicken meat just before it goes bad, wrapped in rotten leaves. Completely cold, but as broad and sodden as the smells of summer. No, I didn't run away. I sat there, breathing shallowly, waiting. There were voices up on the second floor, men's voices, like blocks of stone clumsily rolling off of a soft bed onto a wooden floor. The door to the room opened and the stairs creaked. Somebody came down to the bathroom and pissed by the open door. Jere. Anica's older son—have I mentioned him? The water gushed and flowed, and the weak fragrance of menthol and soap came through. I closed my eyes. Now he'll come in. I felt how he stopped when he caught sight of me but didn't say a word. He went over to the stove, turned on the gas, and, only then, with his back turned, with that nasal nonchalance of his, he said, "You're late." I opened my eyes. At least to see the back of his head, Hladna, the skull round under his smooth skin, tender like a child's and confident in its inviolability. How could a person not long to grab the pot he was taking just then from the cupboard and bonk him over the head with it? "I was knocked low by tragedy," I said. He turned briefly. "I know," he said, not without sympathy, then went on, as if offering his excuse. "Anica called the hospital a couple of times, but they said you were under sedation." He turned once more, eyeing me carefully. "Time has passed since the crash, Gorana." Again, that tone of the brother, two years older, lording it over me: maybe you were the first to learn to write, master the theory of relativity and logarithms, earn your doctoral degree, but I lost my first tooth before you did, fell in love first, and was the first to drink a beer, so everything you have ever experienced, good and bad, I did first. "What are you cooking?" I asked, to change the subject. "Quinoa," he said, pronouncing the word distinctly, with condescension, as if I had arrived after spending thirty-five years on an island in isolation and had never heard of this miracle food. I gave him that. Let him go ahead and rattle off the list of amaranth, bulgur, spelt, adzuki and mung beans, white and borlotti beans, tapioca, millet, and all the legumes, let him lose himself in the flour ground from almonds, buckwheat, rye, oats, chickpeas, and coconut, in the algae and sprouts, as long as he doesn't ask me what I've been up to these last six months. He sat at the table with his gruel and eyed me warily between bites. "So, where's your suitcase?" he asked. "I left it in a locker at the terminal," I said without blinking. "I didn't like the look of the taxi drivers, so I decided to come on foot. And you know my bags never have those little wheels." He chuckled. He thought of me as odd in an eccentric sort of way, and he liked it when I said things that reinforced his idea of me. Then it hit him. "The terminal? Why didn't you drive?" Can you believe it, Hladna? Only then did I remember, at that very instant—I own a car! A red Ford Puma, permanently parked in an underground garage near my apartment. Only a year old, scarcely ever driven. It's got to be worth, I thought, at least 100,000 kunas, at the very least, 70,000. I'd agree to 50,000. I started digging through my bag, looking for the keys. How could I have been so stupid all this time, I fumed to myself, to have so much money right there in front of my nose and not take it. Jere watched me, waiting for an answer. "In for repairs," I said, sounding unconvincing. I knew he'd already seen my confusion and the blush rising on my cheeks. The keys, of course, were not in my purse; they'd been left in the apartment. I forced myself to keep my gaze focused on the spoon that was traveling from the bowl of gruel to Jere's mouth. "You could fix me a little something," I said, intentionally stern, "a cup of coffee, at least, plenty of sugar." He was quiet, watching me with his always slightly startled eyes. "You know where it's kept," he answered at last. I felt a surge of relief. This meant he'd now subject me to a long-winded lecture on the harmful effects of sugar, so I sat back in the chair and dozed with my eyes open, nestling into the gentle tones of Jere's voice like into a soft pillow. How that man droned on, my Hladna. He jumped from the theme of a healthy life to his job at the nursery school, from the nursery school to the theory and history of punk, and from punk to a detailed rundown of Milka's medical care. Former punk rockers like him are the worst. They feel compelled to bring things together with the same fervor they once smashed things apart; even if the puzzle is missing a piece, they'll force any old thing into the space to make the picture whole. I noticed he had recently decided to grow out his hair and a beard; brown whiskers were sprouting all over, uncomfortable on his light skin like the liver spots that come with old age. Now, when he sat, the natural sturdiness of his body took second place to the small head on his fledgling neck; his sweaty forehead, endearing in its fragility like an egg; and his flat nose, which gave him a conciliatory air. I grew more willing to listen to him, or at least watch him while he talked. As he spoke of Milka's condition, he piled on the grim details. He was trying to get under my skin, I knew this; I could see it clearly in his burning eyes and the faint smirk. He boxed my ears with Milka's flaccid limbs, stuffed my nose with her shit and urine, humiliated me, the daughter who'd left her mother in the lurch, but when he paused between sentences and rested his eyes on Milka's prone body, he grew solemn; a darkness welled in his eyes, as if something heavy were sinking into dark water, and I knew he was actually saying, "Lucky you, you left, but I had to come back to our folks when my girlfriend dumped me, and now I'm deep in Milka gruel, like quicksand." Did the kitchen darken a little more just then? Or did the dwindling light of the advancing day, as the little windows indirectly hinted, heighten the gloom? The stairs creaked as Katarina came down in her pajamas, her face puffy from sleep. She glanced at me with curiosity. "Kata! Since when do you wear glasses?" I asked brightly, teasing her. "Since last autumn," she said. What was it that made me so sad about her words? Was it the way she said them, too polite, too reticent, as if talking with an older friend of the family or a relative she was meeting for the first time? Or that she looked right at me as she said them? If she had looked over at Milka or Jere, or if she'd reached for the coffeepot while we were talking, if she'd ignored me the way we ignore those who matter most to us, I'd have felt better.

I'd know: she has thought of me now and then over the last two years. Yet it was as if she'd never been the little girl who grew up by my side, who spied on me and read my diary in secret; the girl I bought Snjeguljica ice cream on a stick and Puc Puc candy fizz for, and brought dresses and books from Zagreb. "What would you like to eat?" Jere asked her while she poured herself coffee. "Nothing, coffee'll do," she said. He shook his head, but he didn't give me any sort of look. "You've got to eat something," he said, "come on, make eggs for yourself and Gorana, or the oatmeal with cocoa you like." He said my name as if signaling to her: Look, this strange architect is sitting here, just in from Zagreb, so why does she have to know you have an eating disorder? She sighed but did what he said. She put water on and then sat at the foot of Milka's bed and tenderly rubbed her grandmother's feet under the covers. A touch that was both condescending and full of a granddaughter's need for her grandmother's attention. Milka shifted her position for the first time. Had she really smiled, or had a shadow flitting over her face tricked me into thinking she had? I thought about what to say. They were so near me. Katarina's smell—fresh, earthy, warm, like newly mown grass on which the sun was drying the dew—tenderly masked the uncomfortable fact of Milka's dying, and I felt I should somehow prove I'd seen her, but before I managed to come up with how, she got up, put eggs in water, and leaned on the stove, watching the back of Jere's head and listening very closely to what he was saying, though she had undoubtedly heard it all many times before. When she moved, I could see she had already picked up some of her mother Anica's slow mellowness, something soft-skinned and kind in her hands and tired in her hips, but now, as Katarina stood there, I saw that she didn't have what flowed with pride and substance from Anica's full head of curly hair to her breasts and the soles of her feet—even as a woman, Anica possessed the air of assurance some little girls display. Katarina's lesser version of the curly hair that runs in our family was very light brown, and her jutting chin and lower lip were more pronounced, as if she were holding back something painful in her jaw, something hard to say, and when she glanced for a moment to the side, her sleepy lashes revealed that she wasn't really listening to Jere. The eggs came to a boil, and I counted off the seconds to myself. One hundred. One hundred fifty. Two hundred. If only she'd take out the eggs in the next thirty seconds, I thought. Two hundred twenty. Two hundred twenty-five. Two hundred forty. If I were to take them out now, I thought, she and I would be saved. It still wasn't too late for them to be soft-boiled. If I were to say, "Do you remember that time during Carnival week?" And if she were to flush red, brighten up, and admit, "Of course!" And then if Jere, snarky but well-meaning, were to add, "Ah, you two." Then, together, we'd laugh and take the time to recall how Kata, not wanting to destroy perfectly good egg yolks and whites during Carnival the way other kids did, once brought hard-boiled eggs with her to throw at houses, with the plan of going back later when nobody was looking to pick them up, bring them home, and eat them, but then cooked them for too short a time, so when she pelted the houses with them, they were soft and the yolks smeared all over. That was our Kata: always striving for perfection and always suffering the consequences. Or was my memory playing tricks on me? I watched as she took her seat at the table, bringing a dish full of eggs and two small plates with silverware. She seemed in sync with her own movements and the space around her, as if she weren't at all sorry she'd dropped out of her studies and come back to her folks. I pulled up my chair. The eggs were hard-boiled. I peeled them, broke them into pieces, and salted them. She set out cheese and tomatoes on the table. Hladna, you cannot imagine how thin she'd been while she was studying medicine in Zagreb. Why had I seen her only twice during those three years? Why didn't I take better care of her? We got together, both times, by the student dormitory on the banks of the Sava. She was like a little bird in the snow, in her thick white coat and oversized cap, but I couldn't remember why I was prepared to abandon her there to expire in the cold. Out of fear? Or simply neglect? I devoured the eggs the way the hungry gobble down food, but the chunks had trouble getting down my throat. The cheese was fragrant. Its white color perfectly matched the color of the plate it was sitting on, so the cheese looked like a vulnerable patch on the plate, a soft hump exposing the fake compactness of the ceramic. Droplets of water, momentarily tense, burst and slid along the unnaturally even skin of the tomatoes. And the others across the table from me—I could hear how the seeds crunched between their teeth and slid down their gullets, only to come out again later. All this was so stupid, so pointless. So horrible, Hladna. I put down my fork and covered my eyes with my hands. "What's up?" asked Jere. "Nothing," I said. I dropped my hands. "It is a fucking furnace in here," I said, trying to sound upbeat. They looked at me, more surprised than concerned. I got up, thinking for a moment about collecting my things and going, but then I said, "I have to pee." I locked myself in the bathroom, sat on the toilet, and tried to pull myself together. "Remember why you're here," I whispered. But no matter how hard I tried, I couldn't convince myself that there had ever been a clear goal for me to achieve. I'd set my apartment on fire, then teenagers were partying around the Meštrović Pavilion, and then I went to the bus terminal and bought a ticket. That's what happened. What lay beneath this, what logic I was following, was beyond me. The police would find me, regardless, and even if I were to muster the courage to ask for some, there was no money in this house for me to cadge. Why was I here, then? I counted the number of toothbrushes in the glass. Five. Not four. Jere's son was living with them now too. His mother had brought him up from Kosovo five or six years before and left the boy with his father, who until that very day had never met him. I tried to figure out which of the toothbrushes was the boy's, but they were identical, except for Dragan's, which looked as if it had been well used at some point but no longer. I was comforted: one of the other four toothbrushes might be mine. I scanned the room. Everything looked the same as always. Reddish-brown tiles below, light-blue ones above. The peeling bathtub. The too-small sink. The mineral scaling on the faucet. The mirror that was missing a piece, though nobody could remember how it had been broken. The claustrophobic sense of safety of a room with no windows. The narrow shape always reminded me of the interior of a ship container. Whenever I sat on that toilet, I always felt as if I were on a journey, and that when I emerged I would be arriving at a new destination. I got up and stood in front of the mirror. My makeup hadn't smeared, but by now, it couldn't hold the face that was pushing its way out. I found some cotton balls, dipped them in lotion, and stripped away the powder, rouge, and lipstick. Then I moved up toward my left eye to wipe off the mascara and eye shadow, but stopped. I knew what my unadorned eyes would look like: exposed in all of their vulnerable warmth, without the help of this mask of ominous blackness. If I stripped the makeup from my eyes, I knew I'd be tired and sad; I wouldn't be able to get through the day ahead. I tossed the dirty cotton balls into the wastebasket, drank a glass of water, and came out. Jere was cooking a pot of porridge; Katarina was gone. The table was already clean. "I threw out the rest of your egg," he said, aiming for indifference. "Where's Kata?" I asked. "She went to take an exam. She's a student again," he said, a little anxious, and added, with a faint scoff, "Culture and tourism." "What the hell?" I said. "Better that than working in retail," he said, and then straightened up slightly as if he'd just woken up, turned off the burner, and moved the porridge to the table. "I'm going out for a smoke. You know how to feed Granny the grits, don't you?" He didn't sound as if he were teasing me, but still I angrily hissed, "She's my mother, isn't she?" He shut the door behind him, and I sat down again by the head of Milka's bed. The porridge was cooling on the table. If it hardened, this would get trickier. I cautiously pulled the pot closer and stirred. How difficult could it be? Scoop up some on the tip of the spoon and coax it into her mouth. As if feeding a child. It didn't seem so challenging. But when I spooned the first mouthful between the half-open jaws, it dropped into her mouth like sand falling into a pit and she didn't budge. "Come on, Mother," I whispered.

"Swallow." "Come on, Milka, hon." "Swallow it, Milky-Way." I shook her shoulder, too gently for her to recoil as she did, inhaling sharply and wheezing, as if the porridge had plugged her airways. This scared me. For a moment, I thought of calling Jere or Dragan, but my old vanity kicked in. Dying is so hard, Hladna. There is no longer any living movement capable of shifting pain over onto other beings and things, yet no blessed release from matter. Pain makes itself at home in the body, and to anybody who tries to oust it, the pain announces: I'm stronger. For some twenty seconds, maybe half a minute, I thought I wouldn't be able to do this, but then her body took pity on me and raised itself a few centimeters, just enough to land the mouthful in her throat in such a way that it could slip down her gullet. I breathed a sigh of relief and wiped my sweaty forehead, but I was still so flummoxed for a few moments that I almost sat on a pot that had been left on the chair. My knees buckled. Milka half opened her eyes. It didn't look as if she knew I was there, but still I had the impression that this whole performance was deliberate. "I'll tell you something, Mother, about your beloved grandson, Jere," I began, scooping up a new spoonful and bringing it carefully over to her. "Do you know how he got that son of his? Do you? Of course not. Nobody knows but me." I was being mean, but I couldn't stop myself. Nothing changed on Milka's face, but because of the way she reacted to the spoon in her mouth, I had the sense she was listening. "The boy is now nineteen, right? Well, nineteen years ago, nearly twenty, when you'd just sent me to live here at Anica's, I came home from school one afternoon a little early. They let us out because we were all soaking wet after a downpour." I stopped. If it had been raining, wouldn't I have made more noise when I came into the house? I probably would've stamped my boots to shake off the water, and then I'd have gone into the bathroom, and when opened, that door always gave a little screech. Someone on the second floor surely would have heard me moving around, and they'd have locked Jere and Ante's room, and I wouldn't have been able to climb up without a sound and see what I saw. So why did my memory tell me there had been a downpour? Maybe because my whole body felt a terrible, cold lightness that day, almost like the sort of joy you feel when the sky cracks open and cries, drenching you to the last millimeter. Why? "Ante was off at a checkup, I think, maybe because of his flat feet, or Dragan had taken him to the island to prune the olive trees. Anica was working the afternoon shift at the hospital. Kata was at school or playing at a neighbor's house. So, do you know what your Jere was up to? He and two of his buddies were fucking a girl from Kosovo." I could still see the girl's bleached hair hanging over the edge of Ante's bed, her oily forehead and large nose, her spilled breasts with dark nipples and her thighs, between which Jere's wiry friend with tattoos was wading as if through water. The other was a burly, pale-skinned guy named Jan, who often hung out here and frequently stayed for dinner. I recognized him straightaway, though all I could see were his bare ass, his back, and the nape of his neck. Jere was standing in the corner, to the right of the girl's head. "Do you know what your grandson looks like naked?" I asked Milka, while she obediently swallowed the gruel. "Different. When he's dressed he may look sturdy, but when he takes his clothes off you see that chicken-like ribcage of his and the sloping shoulders." I remembered

BEDBUGS

the erection, as if artificially grafted onto his body, not participating in the excitement but hanging a bit loose from his soft hips and bluish skin. With his left hand he was slowly pulling on his prick, while with his right he reached now and then for the girl's nipples or hair, stroking them, both curious and uninterested, as if they were the limbs of one of those inflatable dolls that when touched make a funny squeaky sound. Every so often she turned her head to Jan to suck on him, but quickly she gave up and went back to staring at the skinny guy who was inside her. Even through the thin crack between the door and doorframe, she looked as if she were performing a boring task. Didn't her skin have a bluish tint? Seems to me that all four of them were, in fact, a little blue. It must have been wintertime, maybe February, and the rooms weren't heated. Is that why I felt cold? Or was it because of their laughter? "Yes, Milka, and the whole time they were laughing." Why did the laughter bother me? "People shouldn't be laughing while indulging in group sex," I said, while delivering the last spoonful to Milka's mouth, and as soon as I said the words, I knew they were true. Laughter suggests distance from an act, and excitement doesn't tolerate distance. If there is laughter, there cannot be real participation. But that's what Jere was like: he invested a lot of effort in appearing to be freethinking, but he'd never really tested his own limits. Freethinking was merely the substance of his vanity, but he didn't have the daring to abandon himself, a daring which, I now know, is the first prerequisite for freedom. "You are on your way to freedom, Mama," I said softly. "I can say that with confidence, I, who witnessed group sex when I was fifteen, and all I felt was a terrible, cold lightness about it. Early on, I saw how freedom is cold. So, so cold. Cold like a cold room that not a single laugh can warm." Milka slowly smacked her lips, time passed, and I sat with the empty gruel pot on my lap and mused—some about that afternoon years ago, some about death, some about how to get my hands on the Ford Puma. Jere hadn't come back. It must have been hours since he'd left, but when he finally did come into the kitchen, he burst in so abruptly that I flinched. "Finished?" he asked a little reprovingly, as if he had heard what I'd been telling Milka. I needed a few seconds to realize he was referring to how I'd been feeding her. "Of course," I said in a conciliatory tone. Was I being overly strict with him? Yes, he laughed during group sex. Yes, he was afraid to push himself to his limits. But who isn't? I myself have come close to freedom, I thought, but only in those moments when freedom came for me, unsummoned, with metal eyes, and took me by the hand to lead me into absolute loneliness. "What about a vegetable stew today, ha?" asked Jere, and then without waiting for an answer, he took the biggest pot out and put it under the faucet. At the front door there was a light knock. Jere didn't say a word. A young couple entered the room with overloaded backpacks: a smallish, bearded guy with strikingly blue eyes and fleshy red lips, a little repellent, and a dark-skinned girl with a tortured look and huge gold earrings that glistened in the semidarkness, like cross-eyes that don't know what to look at first. The boy asked me, "Apartments Mediterranean Dream?" I shook my head. From his chest pocket he took out a strip of paper, read it, and said, "Yes, Mediterranean Dream." "Up," said Jere, lighting the stove. "Upstairs, third floor." Then he told me, "Zorica's tourists. After they pay, she dumps them here at the door and kicks their butt and ours." It took me a few moments to grasp who Zorica was, but as soon as I remembered she was Dragan's sister, I realized the yearslong quarrel over the inheritance must have finally been resolved. "She got the attic," Jere said, adding, "By-dvay, if you thought you'd be sleeping here, not tonight. Your room is now Mediterranean Dream." The tourists picked up their things, and he went on about the melodrama with Zorica. He knew Dragan's usurpation of the family inheritance was indefensible beyond traditional arguments, so he shifted the whole thing to the problem of class. I stopped listening halfway through his first sentence and returned to daydreaming about the red Ford Puma. Jere chopped a carrot. A potato. A leek. Peppers. Rinsed spinach. Threw in lentils. Salted. Peppered. He cooked and stewed. Only then did I realize he was talking about me, and I began listening again. Apparently, the whole family was angry because two years earlier I'd taken down the roof of our house on the island, intending to renovate it, and then went back to Zagreb with the job unfinished, leaving Milka in Anica's care. I remembered this had, indeed, happened, but I couldn't explain my motives. Jere talked and talked, sweaty and aglow in the steam from the simmering pot. "Milka was doing well then. She didn't need care," I said, just to say something cold. The sentence was accurate; still, I knew it was untrue. Milka had always needed care. She was both child and elderly woman, and when she was forced to remain alone on the island, she devoted particular attention to cultivating little complaints; stubbornly she nurtured back pain and blood pressure that threatened to go over the top, inflamed gums and a bad knee—anything to force us from the mainland to stay in regular touch, at least by phone. Steam filled the kitchen; Jere talked and talked. About how I didn't have the right to undertake the renovations on my own, that all these things had made Milka sick, and that the house had now been crumbling for two years. He uttered all this with his familiar nasal apathy, as if he were merely passing the information on, but a hint of secondary rage broke through in places, as if for the past two years the family had been bugging him so much about these things, he was now furious with me. The steam rose and the windows fogged up, but he didn't switch on the hood over the stove. "It's hot as hell, I mean really," I said and got up to take a paper fan from the china closet. I was wet under my arms, under my breasts and butt, on the backs of my knees, in my crotch, between my fingers. I wiped my forehead, but sweat slid down my back from my neck. I paced around the room, waving the fan. Get away from here, get away as soon as you can, was the only thought on my mind. I tried pushing up my sleeves, but they were too tight. The dress felt too narrow for me to run in. I was overwhelmed by something like angry helplessness. How to explain to this nonchalant dimwit that I don't feel I can own everything that Gorana Hrabrov did? That I'm only now learning who I was, and I may never entirely know? The kitchen was hot, and everything I wanted to say turned to water and dribbled with an irritating softness down my skin to the floor, unable to turn into something more solid, into words with which I could defend myself in a manner that would be at least briefly convincing. I believe, Hladna, that this was the first moment when I thought I might be losing my mind. You must understand me: it was hot, sweat was submerging my body, the steam was blurring the room, the vegetables in the pot were simmering, dead and squishy, to enter my agitated stomach, and Jere was talking, talking, talking. So, you can easily imagine, when the front door suddenly opened and Anica appeared on the threshold, bringing a gust of fresh air into the room, why I felt such relief. Kind Anica. Anica with her child's face and the body of a matron. Always, like Milka, a little flushed, but more discreetly, without hints of inner turmoil. Have I told you how blue Anica's eyes are? Not like the sea, no, not enough depth here. Nor like the sharp stabbing of blue flowers into a green meadow. Nor like the flirtatious sparkle of blue stones. No, this was the blue of a late spring sky, when the afternoon goes slipping peacefully by and all is agreeable, from bee to leaf, from pavement to car chassis, from dog hair to human hair, and the melancholy is low-grade and mild, like a funny little cloud appearing here and there on the horizon. She looked at me, surprised, but didn't glower even a little. I hugged her, and she welcomed me and ran her hands down my back with the same characteristic tender gesture she used for her children. I felt myself shaking. "Now, now," said Anica, "we'll all die," probably thinking I was upset about Milka. I wanted to say something, but my lower jaw shook so hard that I gave up and sat down again at the head of Milka's bed. Anica felt her mother's brow, checked her pulse, and stroked her hands. "Are you well today, dear?" she asked. She'd picked up that irritating habit typical of nurses, speaking to patients as if they're morons, but she did so in the gentlest way possible, without shouting in Milka's ear. "Did she eat?" "She did," I said softly. "She ate the porridge." Anica looked at me, mildly surprised, but didn't say anything. She smelled of the bread roll we used to call cake and dunked in our hot coffee and milk. You may be too young to remember it, Hladna, but when I was little you could buy chewy, round rolls and we called them cakes. Ante and I loved dunking them in our hot coffee and milk. That's how Anica smelled, like something forgotten yet precious, simple nearly to the point of banality, yet good in a complex way that was hard to explain. She sat across the table from me. She was already plodding slowly, but while she sat, the smell of her sweat reached my nose and suddenly she looked more tired than I remembered her being. She put her feet on the other chair, laid her left hand on her thigh, and with her right she smoothed the tablecloth. "What's today?" she asked Jere, without much interest. "My turn," he said, without looking around. She rubbed her neck and briefly shut her eyes. "There's your father down by the water, talking with Edi. He'll need to be called in for dinner," she said. "He knows when dinner's on," replied Jere. Anica turned to me and smiled. "Did you see that?" she said, as if I hadn't heard this same conversation many times. "Win any more awards?" she asked without a trace of irony, almost with pride. I felt a calm sense of safety spread through my body. For the next fifteen minutes, she inquired about my work and, obedient, I answered with an easy satisfaction. "Yes," I said, "we were at that symposium early in the year where we presented our award-winning project, and that's where I met Sergej, such a terrific, fascinating guy, a globe-trotter, a painter, a singer, a theologian, a person with many talents. I'm telling you, no surprise the attraction was fatal. Sadly, brief, but I'll remember forever the time I spent with him. When what happened happened, I was forced to give myself a little break, but I can hardly wait to get going with my new projects." I wasn't even thrown off when she said, "And I always thought you'd end up with that Igor fellow of yours. You couldn't finish a sentence without his name." "Of course," I said. "For years he was my sole colleague. We were always together. We developed all of our projects together, so of course I spoke of him." With Anica her mouth was everything, Hladna. She had a small mouth, barely visible, and when she was listening to someone with trust, pursing her lower lip, her eyes seemed even bigger, as if growing with admiration. When I said, "I was absolutely devoted to my job, so of course my colleague was always on my mind," I knew my persuading was overkill, because her lower lip went slack and her eyes lost their shine, but a maternal sympathy began taking over her face, as if she felt a little sorry for me. "Though I'm not saying he's not good-looking, okay?" I added with a nervous smile. She looked at me suspiciously for a few seconds, and then rebounded with a gentle smile. "Judging by the pictures, he is very good-looking," she said, and then nodded to Jere. "Any chance dinner will be done anytime soon? We're waiting." "Yes," I said, "I'm beginning to think we'll end up hungry today." Unexpectedly, this so confused Jere that he dropped his wooden spoon, and I finally began to feel something like familial warmth. Two Hrabrov women against a knucklehead Tičić. "Let's give a hand," Anica said and struggled up out of the chair, opened the cupboard over the stove, chose some of the better plates, and set them on the table. I got up to help her, and she proceeded to choose spoons, napkins, and glasses. Jere grabbed the broom that stood by the door and knocked the ceiling with the broomstick several times. At the front door there was cheery chatter, and a moment later Katarina and Dragan came in. "I don't even need to ask," said Anica, giving Katarina a knowing grin. "Passed," confirmed Katarina with a smile, looking over briefly at me and blushing. Jere opened the window, but there no longer seemed to be any need for air. The kitchen was now brimming with ringing voices that lent it a clear and bright mood, to the point that the room actually began to feel cleaner and lighter. I didn't notice when Jere's son came down and took his place at the table. He didn't look at all like Jere or what I remembered of the boy's mother. He was a swarthy kid with light hair, slender and serious, with a long neck that was so straight, he seemed much taller than he really was. He had one of those opaque, impassive faces, but a sort of jerky restlessness surfaced beneath the lizard-like eyelids when he noticed me watching him. Katarina sat next to him, and Dragan took his customary place at the head of the table. Jere served the pot with the vegetable stew and sat by the new health-food shelves. "And where will we put you?" Anica asked me, holding the armrest of the last free chair. "Sit here," she said, "and I'll pull up a stool." They looked at me over their plates. "No need," I said, and opened the front door to grab Dragan's chair. Anica had already pushed my silverware to the corner of the table, between herself and Dragan. "Leet us prraaay," chanted Jere through his nose, and everybody laughed. This is nice, I thought, sitting here like this among people I know, doing simple things, eating, drinking, laughing, not thinking about anything big or final, just feeling between my teeth the sweetish mellowness of the vegetables, enjoying the softness of

BEDBUGS 77

the bread and the warmth of the other bodies that are alive, still, despite the fact that I hadn't been taking proper care of them. "Dane, do you know Auntie Gorana?" Anica asked Jere's son. The boy looked over at me and shook his head. "How come you don't know her?" asked Jere. "You saw her at Aunt Irma's funeral when you were small." "Smaller," he corrected himself. Dane silently glanced over at me several times, without any hint of recognition. He looked like a big wooden doll, both brittle and unpredictable in movements, shockproof yet frangible. They treated him, how can I put this, Hladna, as if his age were really the same as how long they'd known him. Like he was an unusually precocious, mature six-year-old. Everything they said, whether it was stories I'd already heard many times before about Dragan's memories from his days at sea, or about Anica's experiences at the hospital, or about invoking Jere's or Kata's childhood, had now acquired an entirely different patina. Even when they talked to one another, or to me, it was as if they were talking to him, as if parading for him our family and the world. Anica reported to me about Milka's health, but it was if she were telling Dane, "Listen to what I'm saying about your great-grandmother." My mother was shifting from being my mother to being his great-grandmother. He was the fulcrum around which the family circle moved. All of their movements depended on his movements, and every smile was for him. And the way they called him Dane, when his full name was Danis. I looked at them all together. They were compact, crammed in around the table in a way that suggested they had no need for anybody else. This was their life, this circle, maybe a little too limited, maybe smothering, but certainly rounded out and solid. Whoever was outside this circle was on the outside.

My gaze was drawn to a photograph of Ante and his boyfriend that stood in the china closet, grimy with dust. He left me, I thought, back then, seventeen years ago; he betrayed our secret plan and went off to study in France. Traitor. "How's Ante?" I asked. "Still in Strasbourg," answered Anica. "A designer of lights for the wealthy, an easy life," added Dragan, not without pride. "He never comes home, he's worse than you, Gorana," said Jere. "If you say a word against his boyfriend," said Katarina softly. "I've got nothing against the kid," grumbled Dragan, "but I can't bear it when he buys those tight-fitting shirts. They don't look right on Ante, see. And it's not okay to be kissing in front of Granny." "You couldn't care less about Granny," laughed Jere, "you just don't like that he's gay." "Not true," said Dragan. Then he added, more softly, "It never bothered me that he was a homo, but he shouldn't be behaving like a little fag." It seemed as if the focus of the conversation would shift away from Jere's son into the hipster apartment in Strasbourg where Ante and his boyfriend lived, but Dane suddenly glanced up at the wall clock, shot to his feet, and said, "I'm late for school." Then he grabbed his bag hanging from his chair and dashed out. "Did you take your snack?" called Anica after him, but there was no answer, and the family circle abruptly and visibly began to disperse. "Gotta get to work," said Katarina, and she went upstairs. "A seasonal retail shift at the store, before classes start," explained Dragan. And Anica was already getting ready to go back for the second half of her shift. "Where's Irma's boy, Zoran?" I asked unexpectedly, surprising even myself. I'd like to be able to tell you, Hladna, that I was truly interested in where Zoran, the oldest of my nephews, was. You'd believe me even if I claimed I'd

BEDBUGS 79

brought up his name purely out of despair, to keep the family from dispersing too quickly and leaving me alone with Milka. But this is no place for lies, dearest dear. I can remember the exact moment when I thought of Zoran, long before dinner, while Jere was telling his stories and I had the Ford Puma weighing on my mind. How I could get my hands on it and go about opening it without my key. Then I remembered how Zoran, at the age of eighteen or nineteen, in the late 1990s, did time for stealing cars. "That's what killed your father," Milka always said. I imagined him now, burly and lop-eared, driving toward me in my little red car of salvation, and the question I asked sounded genuinely tender. "Ask your brother," said Dragan with sarcasm. "He hangs out with Zoran's dad." "The hell he does," said Anica in a tired voice. "Our brother likes anyone who's willing to pay for his booze, and Padovan, thank goodness, is no tightwad. It's easy to forget how he treated Irma back in the day." "As if Padovan has the faintest idea where his boy, Zorko, is," said Jere. Dragan went out to have a cigarette, and a little later Katarina rushed down from the second floor, kissed Anica, gave Jere and me a quick wave, and left. Anica came closer and, in the confidential voice Milka had always used to pass on bad family news, said, "Look, I don't know where he is, but what I've heard is that he's living with some crazy woman in Split, an older American, filthy rich." Only then did I realize how much she'd aged. She was nearing her sixtieth and already saying things like "what he did that time to Irma" or "an older American, filthy rich." She got up. "Time to go," she said and threw open her arms, ready for a hug. I got up and embraced her briefly. She no longer smelled of cake in hot coffee with milk, but of antiseptics. "I don't know how long you plan to stay," she said, holding me by the elbows, "but know there is always room for you here." "What do you mean?" asked Jere, as he collected the plates and spoons. "It's Mediterranean Dream upstairs." "Hey, we'll find space," answered Anica. There was something awful in how she said this with baseless confidence. Her care has always been like that, I thought, a reflex, expressed in gestures she learned back in high school, when she came home to the island every day after school to help care for her little brother, Kiddo, care stemming from years of habits that may seem innate, and which never abandon the body yet don't enter the face, her aging child's face that remains untouchable, absent, distant, sweet in a detached, nearly forlorn way. When she said, on her way out, "I'm so glad we had the chance to see each other," it made me want to cry. "And feed Granny," she added as the door was closing. I could hear her yelling something to a neighbor, and then we were alone again: Jere, Milka, and I. "I have the dishes to wash," said Jere, pouring water into a plastic basin, as if I ought to be getting ready to leave. I stood there, unsure. "Will you help me or feed Milka?" he asked. I went over to the sink. As he handed me the soapy dishes to rinse, I noticed he was already dressed for work, wearing tight gray pants and a white shirt with a penguin design and cute suspenders made of eco-leather. Hadn't he been in a tracksuit earlier? When did he have the time to change clothes? Although the old punk-rock boots he had on his feet brought a little stability to the scene, I was nevertheless feeling ever more clearly the encroaching melancholy Mediterranean summer late afternoon. Again, I caught a whiff of Milka's smell. It mingled with the fragrance of the

BEDBUGS 81

vegetable stew which, still heavy in the air, conversed with the vegetable stew in my gut. Soon Jere would be off to the nursery school, I thought, and I'd be left alone with her, and I'd have to feed her the same vegetables I myself had ingested only a half hour before. Your mother will eat you up, pounded in my head. "I have to go. I have to leave," I said, struggling to keep my voice from cracking. A dish slid from my hand and rang as it hit the sink. Quickly, I rinsed my hands and reached for my purse. "Where are you off to, Goga?" asked Jere. He sounded sincerely surprised. And he used my nickname, Goga. The family name nobody had called me for such a long time. I stopped and turned. He was standing with his hands in the soapsuds, looking at me quite seriously. His gaze, Hladna, how to describe it? There was a touch of concern in it, a touch of sympathy, a touch of anxiety, a touch of tenderness, but there was also a little healthy coldness, as if he were seeing me naked but with no thrill at all. The only person who looked at me that way was Igor. Igor. Igor, I realized, was the only person who saw me as I truly was. He appeared right there before my eyes, as he'd been at the symposium in January, when I spotted him during my talk, standing next to where the audience was seated. What was I saying? I remember saying, "Typical capitalist architecture is architecture that doesn't consider the person. The task of office buildings is to make us uncomfortable about being people." And, "Those buildings made of mirrors on the upper floors reflect the sky and multiply the surrounding commercial context, creating a screen for what's going on inside, a magnificent image making us always too diminutive as we enter, cruelly faced at the entrance by all the humiliating details of our human failings." I remember how Joško Dulčić, the elderly architect who introduced me, was wetly sucking his tongue behind my shoulder. The smell of mothballs from his brown socialist suit frayed my nerves. By then had I already spent the night with Sergej? On January 31 we were married and left on our trip, but the symposium began on the twenty-fifth. We must have met, but did I already know I'd be walking away from everything? Or was it Igor's gaze that spurred me on? Why was he looking at me that way, Hladna? "Why are you looking at me that way?" I asked Jere. I must have sounded stern, because he choked back his words. I ran my wet hand over my hot brow and neck. I looked over at Milka, who was dozing peacefully. "I have to find Zoran," I mumbled and out I went. The day's mild, fresh brightness took me by surprise. Even on the narrow cobblestone street, always in shadow, I could feel how agreeable the weather was. Dragan was nowhere to be seen. The afternoon was as quiet and empty as only Mediterranean afternoons can be. Stirring again—I could feel it—was my animal drive to evade danger. Stick to the narrow side streets, I told myself. But I hadn't advanced even fifty meters before I heard a man's voice calling my name. I turned and saw Jere hurrying toward me. "Gorana, you have a call!" he shouted. I took a step toward him and then a step back. "Your landlord is calling from Zagreb, says it's urgent," he said more softly, coming quite close. I froze. Could I ever have imagined my landlord would come looking for me at my sister's house? When and why had I given him her number? Or had he found her in the phone book? No, that wasn't possible; he couldn't have known her last name. Or did he? "Come on," said Jere, "he's waiting on

BEDBUGS

the line." Hladna, those were several of the longest seconds in my entire life. If I answered his call, I knew I would no longer be Gorana Hrabrov, professor of architecture, award-winning architect, and there wouldn't even be Goga, daughter, sister, aunt, but only a woman who set someone's apartment on fire and ran away. If I go back now to Anica's house, this will all be over. I'll be able to take off this awful dress and the ballet flats that are giving me a backache and throw away being Gorana Hrabrov. "I . . ." I managed to say. Then nothing. "Tell him . . ." "I bet he's calling me for . . ." Freedom is a terrible thing, I'm telling you, Hladna; in freedom there is no hug from Anica or Jere's warm vegetable stew, only an infinite series of cold eyes, from now until death. Behind my back there was a tangle of streets I knew my way around, and beyond them the red Ford Puma and Zoran, who'd know how to open it without a key, maybe even how to sell it fast on the black market. With that money I could pay a snappily dressed attorney, someone who would know how to convince a judge and my family that it was purely by chance I'd forgotten to put out the candle. People believe in fancy suits and polished shoes, in leather briefcases and Swiss watches. People fall for things like that, right? It's always possible to get away with things, right? To reembrace my name and get on with my life. I decided—don't hold it against me—to cling fervently to that possibility, though I was on my last pair of panties and I was sure that my downfall was a certainty. "Tell him I'll call him on my cell," I finally managed. Watching me, Jere asked in a serious tone, "Are you okay, Gorana?" He came closer. "If you're in trouble of some kind, say so. We're family," he added with gentleness. I realized he'd spotted the red marks on my hands.

"Everything's fine," I said, "everything is in the best possible order, I'd just like to see Zoran, that's all." I turned to leave. "Tell Mr. Zagreb I'll give him a buzz," I said, trying to sound breezy, though I could hear something in my voice that was a little like the restlessness of treetops before a summer storm. I also added, as I walked away, "I'll be back." Then I picked up the pace. I didn't turn to see whether he was still watching me.

I cut across the center of town, taking side streets I knew would be almost completely empty at this hour, hopped on a bus, and rode it to the bus terminal. A second bus, the one that went to the outskirts where Kiddo lived, was already at the stop. I got on and sat across from a woman. At first it was half empty, but kids began piling in on their way home after the morning shift at school, and soon there was hardly any standing room left. A dark-haired, wiry old man came in through the back door, dragging his feet behind him; he worked his way in among the kids, remarking something to each one, and ended up right next to me. He took hold of the pole and stopped talking. The bus pulled away, and I remembered I didn't have a ticket. The bus was getting stuffier and hotter. The old man said a few words to each person near him—the kids smirked at his remarks and the tired middle-aged women responded politely—but when he turned to face me, he fell silent. The woman across from me sat quietly with her huge belly, surrounded by overflowing plastic bags, which gave the impression that she had no intention of moving, but as the swelter mounted, her face became oilier and broadcast a sort of internal distress, as if sitting imposed an unpleasant obligation on her. I felt I should sit, yet I also felt I should stand. At the third or fourth stop, an older man got on, smooth-shaven, with a thick neck and sharp gaze. He peered sourly around the bus. I froze. He headed straight for me, and there I was, terrified, with no ticket. For a few seconds I didn't know what to do. Suddenly he smiled, and I realized he'd recognized the old man who was standing right next to me. "Viva Duce!" exclaimed the newcomer. I breathed a sigh of relief. "Viva Italia!" replied the old man. They embarked on lively banter, and I turned to face the window and have a look at the outskirts of town as the bus passed through them. The next stop was supposed to be the right one, if any stop could be right. Is there a need, Hladna, for me to describe the incoherence of the region I was entering? Still, despite the impossible scenography, in the eclecticism of the various levels of kitsch, in the unconscious reliance on the Brutalist style and hyperboles of every variety, there was something human, touching in its awful imperfection. I left the main road, crossed over to the north side, and, for a few seconds, was torn about which street to turn into. It was only after a few hundred meters, when the pavement switched to macadam, that I was sure I was walking in the right direction. Cars seldom passed, but each one that drove by raised such a hot cloud, I could barely breathe. A marvel of dust caked my sweaty skin. I was thirsty. My arms itched from the traces of the bedbug bites. You'll understand, then, why I was so overjoyed to see my brother's hideous house, a red-block building, Frankenstein additions annexed to the existing structure with the birth of each new child, never completed, no roof or windows on the upper floor. On the concrete front path sat a boy of about ten, playing with pebbles and talking to himself. I crouched down beside him.

"What are you making?" I asked. I couldn't remember his name. I knew he was their third, their youngest, but I had only seen him in photographs. He looked at me and blushed. He had blue eyes like his mother's, but not as big, cold, or dependent on what they were reflecting, like a reflecting water surface. Instead, his were like something precious buried in sand, two firm points on his face, a face that was changing from one second to the next, unsure of whether to introduce itself with its freckles, curly hair, round chin, pink lips, or big ears. "It's a shopping center," he said, a little hurt, averting his eyes. Gracia came to the threshold with a kitchen towel in her hand. "Who's that you're talking to, Davor?" she asked. The question voiced surprise at seeing me, but her face remained wholly impassive. "Gorana," she said, "where did you come from?" And then, without waiting for an answer, she added, "The gentleman of the house, your brother, is at the table. The man required a little time off after dinner." Her lips barely moved when she spoke, and everything she was saying sounded as if she had to yank it with effort from between her jaws, or straight from bone, from her squarish, rock-hard chin. She was even skinnier than I'd remembered, but she had acquired a new toughness that, despite signs of age—her salt-and-pepper hair and wrinkled neck—gave her a suppler, younger look. She went back inside, and I followed her. We crossed the front hall in two steps and entered the kitchen, the first door to the right, just as I'd recalled. "There, have a look at him," she said, nodding at my brother, Ivan— for me, he'd always be Kiddo— who was sitting at the table, a cigarette in one hand and a glass in the other, staring blankly into space. He glanced over at me, then took a drag on his cigarette. He had adopted our father

Mate's smoking style but lacked Dad's authenticity. Mate used to honor his cigarette by bringing it to his lips, always with a frown of dissatisfaction, and while Kiddo's gesture was exactly the same, the smoke took control in the end, as if taunting him for his habit; this made his weak physique seem weaker yet. Here, too, the difference was in their eyes: Dad's small black eyes were naturally planted in his robust face, while on Kiddo they looked unconvincing, as if on the basis of his borrowed eyes someone had haphazardly, last minute, slapped together Dad's son. Hence his every movement came across as a poorly learned lesson. "Have a seat, Gorana," said Gracia. Even that simple sentence sounded like a reproach leveled at Kiddo. I took the nearest chair, to my brother's left. The kitchen was much as I remembered it. The work area behind the bar, tongue-and-groove siding in the dining area, the national coat of arms as the only picture. The unpleasant smell of the damp and walls stained black with mildew. Not a single plant, no magnets on the refrigerator. Gracia went over to the sink and continued briskly washing dishes. "So, you've come, have you?" remarked Kiddo. Then he did that half-circle thing with his eyes and his unique shoulder shrug, conveying, You just show up here as if nothing happened, so what have I got to say to you now? "Oh, fuck this," he said, inhaling his words with the smoke, as if to himself. I decided to let him talk. Davor sat down across from us, watching me with curiosity. In his eyes there was a compassionate tenderness that I clung to, assuming the posture of remorse, while I listened to Kiddo accuse me of the demise of the family, the fall of the house of Hrabrov. Did I not take the roof off our house and abandon the place to ruin? I did. Did I behave as if the legacy were mine when it was supposed to be his? I did. Was I always dissatisfied? I was. Had I pretended to be smarter than I really was? I had. I knew that if I were patient enough, I'd surely find a way to steer us toward Zoran and my Ford Puma. Kiddo was like that; he tried to sound tough and wise like Dad, but he wasn't nimble enough to finish his thoughts. Inevitably he'd bog down in contradictions; he'd begin by mentioning people and events that had nothing to do with his central idea, and, ultimately, he'd simmer down, embrace his drink, and leave others to steer the conversation wherever they liked. Already he was showing the weakening of his resolve. He expanded the story about my childhood to include the story of his friends back then and their lives today, but before I managed to find an opportune gap in the conversation into which I might insert Zoran, a tall, good-looking girl barged into the room and, paying no attention to me, stretched her hand out to Kiddo and said, more as statement than question, "Hey, Old Man, got a smoke." This had to be Maša, whom I'd last seen at Irma's funeral when she was a girl in early puberty. She still had some of her then sporty physique, but she'd filled out in a nice way. Her face was longer, and her full lips gave greater emphasis to her expression of all-powerful superiority. "Who's this?" she asked, nodding at me. "Aunt Gorana. Don't you recognize her?" said Kiddo, giving her a look of paternal tenderness and pride while she ran her tongue along the cigarette and lit it. "Aha," she said, exhaling her first puff of smoke, "the Zagreb one?" Her eyes, quite cold until then, sparked interest. "How is it you say shit up there?" she asked. I was thrown off. She grinned, exposing bad teeth. "I'm fucking with you," she said. She sat across from Kiddo to my left and put up her feet on the table edge. "Maša," protested Gracia, while rinsing the dishes. How did she manage to make everything she said sound like a reproach aimed at Kiddo? "What now?" snapped the girl edgily. Then she turned to me. "Married?" she asked. "Nope," I said. "Boyfriend?" I shook my head. "No traffic, eh? So, what do you do all day?" "Work," I said. "I'm an architect." "Wait, are those the guys who go digging around in the bones?" It irritated me how she was pushing me to sound superior. "No," I said as neutrally as I possibly could, "those are archaeologists. Architects make the drawings that engineers and builders use to build buildings, like houses or schools or hospitals." "If only you architects hadn't done the drawings for my school building," she said, flashing Kiddo a conspiratorial grin, "maybe then I wouldn't have flunked second grade." "Gorana is a doctor of architecture," said Kiddo with the same sort of grin, emphasizing the word "doctor," as if making light of it. "You don't say, a doctor! Know any famous docs, like House or McDreamy?" "No," I said patiently, "I'm not that kind of doctor. I wrote a doctoral thesis about the influence of Le Corbusier on Yugoslav postwar architecture." "Ah, I'm fucking with you," she said a little wearily and exhaled smoke, as if I were the one who didn't get it. Lounging in her chair, she pulled up her top and started picking at her belly button piercing, giving Kiddo the floor and eyeing me from a new distance, as if trying to suss me out. Kiddo grumbled on about the house on the island. What he could have done but for my reckless behavior. He could have been going there every weekend. Cultivating the olive grove and producing olive oil for sale. Looking after the boat. Having a peaceful place for his retirement. "Cut it out, Old Man, you're so full of shit," interrupted Maša. "Olives? Give me a break!" She took her feet off the table and shot him a sharp glance, not so much with her eyes as with her pencil-thin eyebrows. "What you should be doing is building vacation apartments, that's where the money's at," she said, rapping the table a few times with the fingers that were pinching her cigarette. Gracia snarked from the kitchen sink, "This gentleman has retirement on the brain, but he has, like, twenty more working years to go. And how will he earn his pension when his work is mostly under the table? When he works, that is." He didn't say a word. He took a sip of his drink and stared blankly, his face showing more wrinkles. There was something immeasurably sad in his hair. Although it had thinned, he was still combing it back, "Italian" style, like he'd done in the 1990s. I thought, I should mention Zoran now, now when he's weaker. Now's the time. But no matter how I tried, I couldn't tear my eyes away from my brother's grimy fingernails, his fingers that trembled ever so slightly with every move he made, and the words in my throat felt like fluttering butterflies, dry and miserable, condemned to die. "So, what are you up to these days, Kiddo?" I asked. He was quiet for a bit, before saying, "Body work on cars, like always." "Here in my garage," he added. Turning to Gracia, Maša went on to explain why building vacation apartments was so important, but soon she was interrupted by a gangly, stooped young man with a doltish, arrogant sneer, who strolled into the kitchen, paying attention to no one, went over to the girl, whispered something in her ear, and flashed her his phone. She became serious, dropped her cigarette into the ashtray, and went with him to the farthest corner of the kitchen to engage in a hushed conversation. I looked over at Kiddo with a questioning raise of the eyebrows. "Mate Junior," he said faintly, mocking but not without pride. "Don't you recognize your nephews?" he added with mild disdain. His strength was reviving. He launched back into talk of the legacy. Hladna, that man could flog a subject without end. Ivan "Kiddo" the Landless Man. He had spent his whole life at this table with a drink and a cigarette, talking about imagined riches that would one day be his. I tried looking at little Davor, his angelic eyes and freckled face, sweetly solemn while soaking up his father's every word. The boy would look over at me from time to time, and, for no reason, he'd shoot me a big grin; the half-moon of his teeth would exude a premature scampishness, and his expression would transform into the flushed face of the most ordinary of street urchins, stripping me of my defenses when facing off against my brother's subtle aggression. And the two knuckleheads in the corner. Did they have to be talking as if something were there, beneath the surface, that couldn't make its way out? A person has to despise teenagers at least a little, as I'm sure you'll agree, Hladna. Kiddo spun tales about distant family history. About Granddad Mate, Mate's father, who returned from fighting for the partisans in the war without one of his legs, yet he was still able, when playing bocce, to hit the jack, the *bulin* as we call it, from thirty meters away. About Granny Palma, whose five children died, but she was still able to dance on tables during village festivals and weddings. About the other grandfather and grandmother. About Mate's sudden death and Milka's imminent demise. Their pain was all my fault. I had hurt them with my unreasonable urge to behave like a man.

I and only I. Don't laugh, Hladna, if I say that my throat was as parched as if full of dead butterflies. I don't know how else to describe for you the dreadful dryness his stolid words sprayed me with. Everything became so fragile. The plastic flowers on the tablecloth wilted under my fingertips and I heard the sawdust a worm was making inside the tongue-and-groove siding and the paper wings of flies flapping mid-flight. The disintegrating threads in the fabric, the floury peeling of skin, the wooden eyelash that dropped from my face to the floor. "Coffee, Gorana?" asked Gracia. Her voice sounded scattered. Surrounded by the black mildewed walls, she looked as if she were battling soot that was about to drown her. Only her eyes flashed like wells. "Water," I croaked. "A glass of water, please." Mate Junior left without a goodbye and Maša came back to the table, but our conversation no longer held any interest for her. She put her feet back up and fiddled with her piercing, saying, "Shit," softly, over and over, chuckling to herself, but when she took a drag on her cigarette, her face went stiff with solemnity, the source of which, as was visible, was far from everything around her just then. I felt this was the ultimate moment to inquire about Zoran, but first I had to pull myself free of the sand the floor was turning into, and my glass of water was not forthcoming. "Dad was a Gothic cathedral," I said out of the blue, flinching from what, monumental and terrifyingly sharp, I had raised among us. Kiddo protested. "Yes," I said, tentatively and implacably, as if walking right up to the door of Notre-Dame, "Mate was like a Gothic cathedral. A person, like me, may not believe in God, yet can nonetheless admire the conviction with which the Gothic cathedral insists that God does exist. There is something gorgeously honest in the absolute trust with which the builders approach the stone and glass, the confidence with which they express their illusion. Mate was like that." Kiddo said nothing, instead squinting out from the double bags under his eyes. "And you," I went on, now more sure of myself, "you are like the neo-Gothic. There can be a modicum of success in form, but the neo-Gothic does not exert power over people through what it is, but through the oblique aggression of how it leans toward what it aspires to be. The neo-Gothic church does not believe in God, but strives to convince the faithful that God exists." Coldly, I added, "How can one fail to despise such buildings?" There was a hush. Gracia fiddled with the pots and did not bring me my glass of water. "There were times when I was afraid of Dad, but mine was the fear of being faced with a force of nature: there was always a safe space for me to retreat to. You knew he was barely literate, and there was so much beyond his ken. There, in the realm beyond the reach of his thinking, that's where I used to hide." Silence. Sand in mouth. The clatter of pots sharp and painful like the afternoon sun. "And you, you did not behave with the innocence of a natural disaster, out of your own strength that had no need to fear others, no, your need to treat me like a stern father comes from weakness. You needed my fear so you could grow up. You think I didn't know how you dogged my every step, like Big Brother, when I moved to the city? How you frightened Milka with even my most harmless choices? You made every street in that city a source of anxiety for me. At every window there was somebody who might accuse me." Then, speaking in the local dialect to make it hurt more, I said, "When Papa died, they told me he'd succumbed. I remember. I came back that afternoon from school, and Aunt Mara and that other aunt, the one with the double chin, were standing outside the front door. That's exactly what they told me: 'Yer poppa, he succumbed.' I can't say there was no relief in this for me, that the horizon didn't seem suddenly unfettered, but how can a person not be overwhelmed by a terrible sadness, despair, really, when a Gothic cathedral falls? When you die—and you won't for many years—everyone will say you croaked." I felt a hush settle over us, the kind of silence that develops around someone who has died. Maša looked at me as if she were seeing me for the first time, a person to be approached with a healthy dose of trepidation. Gracia came over to the bar to have a closer look. Davor sent each of us, one by one, a questioning glance. If only Kiddo had raised his voice then. If he'd interjected something poisonous about my brief stint with my Serbian husband or my lack of care for Mother. But no, he clenched into himself even more tightly in his pitiful yellowed shirt and said very softly, as if to himself, "So, I guess . . ." I wanted to tell him to quit it. He was no victim. Let him save that story for his buddies at the betting shop. Oh, Hladna, my friend, if you could have seen the way he turned to Davor, smiling woefully, and said, "Hear this, child?" you'd understand why there was nothing left for me to say. Maša said something to Gracia; Gracia asked Davor a question. Nobody looked at me, but in each of their words there was inner warmth and external coldness, as if they were raising their shields before me. What I'd said was left dangling in midair, falling slowly and crumbling, and believing it to be true was getting more and more difficult. Hadn't I myself been unsure of my own

BEDBUGS

affective memory? Wasn't I speaking out of despair, because of my own ineptitude at finding my way to Zoran and the Ford Puma? My throat was achingly parched. I grabbed the bottle of wine that was on the table and downed a long gulp. Nobody told me to go, but clearly their hospitality was over. Maša stubbed out her cigarette, and without a goodbye she left the room; Gracia went out, muttering that she had to start a load of laundry, and did not come back; and Kiddo put down his drink and cigarette, leaned back, crossed his hands behind his head, looked up at the ceiling, and softly hummed a song I didn't recognize. I rose to my feet. "I'll be off, then," I said. He shrugged, as if to say: your call. I turned and walked through the open kitchen door and the open front door. Only Davor saw me out. After two-three steps along the concrete path I stopped, laid my hand on his shoulder, and leaned over to him confidentially. "Do you know who our cousin Zoran is, Davor? Irma's boy, Zoran?" I asked softly. "Irma died," he said, a little worried. "Yes, I know she died," I said, "but do you know her son, Zoran, the big, muscular guy?" He was quiet for a moment, then said, "Daddy says that clown is either crazy or nuts. Crazy or nuts. And Mama, uh Mama, uh Mama says, 'Don't you let him come in if he stops by.'" The fleshy parts of his ears burned, and his lips were slick with spit. He had the feeling we were doing something bad. "Has he been to visit you here?" "Nope." "Has your Mama or Daddy or Maša or Mate said they ran into him in town?" "Nope." "Good," I said, trying to sound as if I were talking with a grown-up. "Thank you for your help." I turned to go, but stopped when I realized there was still something tickling his throat. "Daddy says," he said and grinned. "Daddy says, 'Who the hell but Jakovčević has any clue where Zoran is.'" And he hooted with laughter. Gracia came to the door. "Ah, Gorana, still here," she said, every bit as impassively as when she'd greeted me. "Davor, come inside." The boy trotted over to her, leaned the back of his head on her chest, and looked at me from this safe distance, protected by his mother's arms wrapped around his shoulders. He was a bit too red in the face and Gracia looked at me warily, as if I were a bad influence and she didn't want me near her boy. I quickly said goodbye. Before I set off down the street, I heard the door shut behind me. Where to now? I went back to the bus stop, sat there, and waited for a time, but finally changed my mind and set off into town on foot, preferring to avoid the ticket inspector. I walked slowly along, running over various possibilities. Although my position seemed hopeless, I no longer felt fear. Only that heavy old loneliness that had nestled into my chest. The sun was waning and the afternoon had achieved a perfect balance between serenity and action. There was a smell of the trees in the yards, the grapes fermenting in the cellars, the soil into which autumn was already advancing. A clear sky, mild air, the pleasant ease of cars and voices. From somewhere came the smell of goulash; somebody was cooking up fruit for canning marmalade. The peaceful lurch of children's swings. Melancholic laughter. The tenderness of birds. I was terribly tired. If there was at least a place, I thought, where I could go to peel eggplants and long red peppers, to cook up batches of ajvar and pickle cocktail onions, cook plums and arrange dried figs in metal boxes with a bay leaf and rosemary. I'd stretch a plaid cloth over the lid on the jam jar and write on the sticker: "Goga's Dalmatian Ajvar." Or: "Goga's Plum Jam. No sugar added."

This made me smile, though there was something too poignant about the thought that I might never again have a chance to put up winter stores. Somewhere at the bottom of my grief, however, lay the feeling that I might still be able to pull this off. I remembered that I probably still had twenty kunas or so after buying the bus ticket in Zagreb. I could go to Jakovčević's in K. to find out where Zoran was, I thought. I took out my wallet and counted out my money. I had twenty kunas in bills and another eight in change. The ticket to there, I thought, couldn't cost more than fifteen, and a return ticket would be just under twice that. I really might have enough. My shoes were chafing me something awful, but I never stopped to think of taking them off; I was reluctant to attract attention in the densely populated part of town I'd already reached, among tall buildings with many windows, stirring, again, my sense of caution. I felt a modicum of relief when, at 5:47, I arrived at the bus terminal, and even more relief when, for only twenty-two kunas, I had my return ticket in hand to and from K. The 5:50 was ready to depart. I fell into a seat at the back of the bus, hugged my bag, and watched how the evening was barely visibly mastering the outer and inner space. So it goes. The blue slipcovers gained in resonance, while the windows, with lavish melancholy, bid farewell to cherished light. The handful of passengers relaxed their shoulders and passersby dragged their feet. The buses pulled calmly and securely out of the bus terminal, without even the slightest premonition that an accident might happen. So it goes. I was off to see Jakovčević in K. to find out where Zoran was, and this was the only thing on my mind. It was only once we'd neared K. that I realized I wasn't exactly sure where Jakovčević lived. I'd been there only twice: the first time after Anastazija was born, when I was about ten, with Mama, Dad, and Kiddo, and the second time in April 2015, when Irma died, and both times I was delivered to the front door by car. I remembered only that he lived on the edge of the village, a little farther inland from the sea, in a small house without a pitched roof. But when I stepped off the bus at the waterfront, I had no idea where to go. From the covered terrace of a nearby pizzeria, in the semi-darkness, I could hear occasional cheery voices and the scraping of chairs, while children yelled and cursed at a soccer pitch on the north side. Otherwise, it was quiet. Lights were turning on in the indigo of twilight, and this gave off a small-town warmth.

I went over to a potbellied old man who was puttering around with nets on his boat, mending and untangling them, constantly fuming—as could be seen both from afar and up close—at a stretch of the net that would not bend to his will. "Good evening," I said in as friendly a voice as I could muster. "Do you by any chance know where Jakovčević lives?" I couldn't remember Jakovčević's first name, so I added, "A widower; his wife's name was Irma." He gave no reaction whatsoever. On he went, mending the nets as if he hadn't heard me. "Jakovčević," I said. "He has two daughters, Đana and Anastazija, and a stepson, Zoran. He works off and on in the building trades." He continued to stay quiet, but even in the yellowish dusk I saw his round face reddening. He could hear me, but for some reason he wouldn't look my way. "Do you know, by any chance, where he lives?" I was not giving up. "It's very important." "I don't know anything," he replied finally, jerking his head briefly as if shooing away a fly, and went on glowering at his nets. As far as he was concerned, the conversation was over. I looked around at the other boats, only just audibly groaning on the calm seas. Nobody in sight. Where are you, passersby? I was reluctant to go to the pizzeria or the soccer pitch. In those places, despite the postseason quiet, there were too many witnesses. Luckily, a petite older woman came out of a nearby store, lugging a huge straw basket from which dangled stalks of leeks. She was dressed as if for Sunday Mass, in a white skirt and floral blouse, neatly coiffed, and her face was well tended and shining. When I approached her and said hello, she inspected me with a courteous interest. "How can I help you?" she asked. She did not speak with a local accent. "I'm looking for Mr. Jakovčević," I said. "Perhaps you know him. He's a widower twice over and has three children. He spent a year or so in the war, and now he works occasionally as a physical laborer." "Aha," she said, looking suddenly serious. For a moment, it seemed like she might turn around and leave. Why did Jakovčević evoke this reaction with everybody? Or was it something about me that was scaring off these people? "There are a lot of Jakovčevićes here," she said, "but I think the man you mean is the one who lives up in the woods. There." She gestured in a general way, first to the northwest, and then at the word "there" she pointed elsewhere, to the northeast, and she headed in that direction right after she said it. "Thank you," I called to her back, which was quickly dwindling. I turned in the direction she'd pointed to, trying to remember Jakovčević's first name. I summoned Dad, Mama, Anica, Kiddo, Maria, and Irma herself from memory, but they always spoke of him as "Her Man." Irma called him "My Man," as if the expectation was that she'd be permanently disgruntled with her husband out of necessity, but she always said it with a poorly concealed tenderness. My nephews, if they mentioned him at all, probably called him "Uncle Jakovčević." What was his name? The dark had almost fully taken hold, and I wandered along the cramped, illogical village streets, without a true sense of where I was going. At certain moments, I had the impression I was alone with the village, the blackened windows of the empty apartments watching me on all sides, but then a larger or smaller tourist group, tanned and wearing light-colored clothes as if this were the middle of summer, walked by on their way down to the pizzeria for dinner, and the evening became irritating, but more ordinary. Once I reached the part of town where the houses were farther apart, I realized I'd never find him if I didn't ask someone else. The occasional car passed; all the drivers looked around my age, and I was afraid some of them might recognize me. I hesitated for a long time, too long, so long I began thinking I'd no longer have anyone to ask. When I came across a young couple who looked like teenagers, pushing a stroller with a little girl in it, only a year and a half or two years old, I felt I'd met people young enough that they wouldn't care who I was. "My apologies for the bother," I said. "Do you happen to know where Miroslav Jakovčević lives?" How had I suddenly summoned his name? Believe me, Hladna, right before I uttered those words, there before my eyes, uninvited yet welcome, came Maria's Omer, who looked at me with his bright eyes, so light in such a dark-skinned face, and said, "Miroslav, may I help you?" Omer, a poor child from central Bosnia whose mother died young; he, who was raised by institutions and outsiders—from the military academy to the Elektra power company—knew how much a name can matter.

And that words are actions. I stood there with Omer at my side, stable and rational once again, and calmly asked where Miroslav Jakovčević lived. The young couple looked at me as if I were their strict teacher. "Miroslav Jakovčević?" the girl said, turning to the boy as if asking him to explain a lesson she hadn't followed. "Miroslav... Miroslav," he repeated, scratching his chin. He was a nervous guy with jerky gestures, and I knew I'd be feeling anxious again soon enough. She sank into her big breasts and puzzled over this. She was really trying. "Oh, right," the girl said to the boy, "isn't that Staza's dad, Uncle Miro?" "Riiiight," he confirmed. Then he turned to me. "He lives up the hill, almost all the way to the woods. Turn left here at this house," he said, pointing behind himself, "and then from the big house with the fountain in the yard, go straight up another two hundred meters or so." "Thank you," I said and smiled, and they responded with big grins. And their little girl even found something hilarious in this. There in the dark, the beautiful white teeth they all had were visible and the evening suddenly began to glow, as if another three moons were shining. Following their directions, I came out right in front of Jakovčević's house. Sunken in darkness, surrounded by tall pines with the pine needles stirring only audibly, the wan streetlamp lit the structure in its roughest contours. The building was shabbier than what I remembered, closely resembling a flat-roofed garage with crooked shutters and a chain-link fence. My stomach clenched. This is it: my one and only chance. The evening will soon cross into night, and I have nowhere to go. I made my way down the trodden path among the brambles to the front door, found the doorbell, and pressed it. No sound; nobody responded. Through the glass pane on the front door, I could see a pale bluish light. I knocked. Three times. Then another three, harder. Nothing. Come on, Jakovčević, I said to myself, you can do this. I took a deep breath and knocked hard. "Miro!" I called. "Irma's Gorana here." I felt someone inside move. Once more I knocked. "Gorana here," I repeated, trying to be loud enough yet also sound peaceful. I waited tensely. I cannot describe to you the relief that flooded through me when a light went on inside and the key turned in the lock. Through the partway opened door peered Jakovčević's broad face. He looked me over with his tiny, frightened eyes. "Gorana," he groaned, "well, welcome. Come in, come in," he added with more cheer and flung the door open wide. Once I was inside, he said, "Will you look at that, you never know whom Jesus might bring to your door." Oh, Christ, I thought, what's this Jesus thing now. I wanted to turn around and walk out. "Sit down," said Jakovčević. "What would you like to drink?" "If you have a glass of water," I said. "Water? Why not try the juice I make from wild blackberries? They grow right here around the house, one hundred percent ecological." "Sure," I said, just to distract him, at least for a moment, from staring at me, to catch my breath, to have a look around the room and adapt. I remembered very little of what it had looked like, yet everything seemed unchanged. The front door opening directly into the living room, no front hall; in the first corner to the left there was a plywood wardrobe, behind that a two-part gray sofa bed with dowdy pillows, and in the middle, a round table covered with a lace tablecloth Milka had made—every evening while Irma was still alive, the table would be pushed into the corner, with the television set to the right, so the sofa bed could be opened up for sleeping. On the wall across from the front door, there was a little yellowish kitchen and the door to the bathroom. On the right wall, entrances to two small children's rooms. A single window. The impression was of the permanently temporal. I sat on the sofa, and Jakovčević handed me a glass of dark-red juice, filled to the brim. When he sat next to me, the surface of the liquid sloshed and nearly spilled over the rim. I took a quick sip. "When did you arrive from Zagreb?" he asked, placing special emphasis on the word "Zagreb," as if referring to a place on Mars. I remembered he'd always greeted me with respect during our rare encounters. When I spoke about my work as an architect, his lips would pucker and purse and he'd watch me, unblinking, rubbing his chest with the broad palm of his right hand, as if trying to stir up within him something he could use to join the conversation on an equal footing. "You see," he said, pointing to several books in a pile on the shoe cabinet that stood beneath the window, "I read and I read. It'll drive us nuts." He'd enrolled at some point in a course of administration studies in Split, and since then he'd been convinced that he was a misunderstood intellectual. It was so easy for him to lie, but the admiration with which he followed my every sentence about architecture irritated me, so I did what I could to turn the conversation to family matters. How's Anastazija doing? Is she recovering? Is she thinking about resuming her studies? What about Đana, Đana's husband, Đana's kids, Đana's hair salon, Đana's mother-in-law, Đana's dog? How are his father and mother, brothers, the brambles in the yard? Irma's photographed eyes watched me from the wall by the television set. Her sensual face on which her features were outsize and too expressive, the face of a teenager who brought home her baby boy, Zoran, born out of wedlock, and, in the eyes of the family, forever went on being a teenager. Silly Irma. Gullible. What does she know? She didn't even finish school. That's not how I remembered her. I remembered her double chin, a little double chin that wasn't visible in the photograph, because you could only see it in profile in those moments when she'd look away to think about something, when the grand emotions from her big lips—always lipsticked— and round eyes with those long lashes and her curly hair, when those emotions slid down to her neck and jostled there, unsure whether to go back up to her face or slide, silenced, to her belly. I wanted to ask Jakovčević about Zoran, but each time I thought the moment right, I'd catch sight of Irma's black eyes, shining in the light of the bare lightbulb that gave them a poignant vitality. "Are you going to exploit your poor nephew so meanly?" her eyes accused me. "Your Zorko, who was an older brother to you until you were ten, when you lived down on the island with Mate and Milka and Kiddo, Zorko who loved you without a word, even though you believed the village stories about him, Zorko who treated only you with no hostility? Are you really going to do that to me? Me, who washed the bare asses of elderly Germans so I could bring you your first bike?" Jakovčević began talking about Jesus, and I knew he'd soon flatten me if I didn't grab the moment, but Irma was there on that wall, looking sadly at her hands and saying, "My skin is starting to flake from the chemo. That's why you don't want to eat my cookies, right?" I froze. The last time I saw her was for Christmas in 2014, a few months before she died, in the house on the island, where, with Milka and Anastazija, she spent her last days, and she really did bake cookies, these crescent cookies with almonds I loved. But, Hladna, how could I not see that the skin all over her body was peeling? This wasn't the ordinary shedding of a membrane, the exfoliation of dead cells; no, this was decay, the fragmenting of the facade, the tearing away of the mask, the allowing of bloody insides to come out. The crescents were tasty, but the more of them I ate, the more I tasted the acrid tang of Irma's skin. Did she notice when I went to the bathroom to rinse out my mouth? Jakovčević was busily interpreting the New Testament for me. He had the bad habit of talking with people he hadn't seen for years as if he saw them every day, speaking right from the heart of the matter with no introduction, but J managed to figure out that he'd joined an obscure Bible study group. Immersed in the topic, he fidgeted with his thickset body on the sofa, hopped up and fell back in feigned awe, sat forward tensely on the edge of the cushion, then sank in when he felt he'd made his point, and the juice in my hand was threatening to spill over the edge, though I kept taking little sips. I had a powerful urge to interrupt him in the sharpest way possible, to say I wasn't interested in anything he was saying, but I didn't dare allow a single drop to fall on Irma's tortured rug, the single item she'd brought with her as a dowry into the house, nearly black from the stains that had built up on it over the years. I nodded and held my tongue. Now, I thought to myself, if he stopped talking for a minute, now would be the right time to mention Zoran. But, again, Irma stepped away from the wall, moved nearer to me though I wouldn't look at her, raised her shirt to show me her amputated breast, and said, "One day you'll be beautiful like this." Or she sadly brushed her hair and her hair broke off. Or she frantically applied makeup, smeared lipstick beyond the edges of her lips to her nose and over her whole forehead, then said, "Am I smart enough for you now?" After a time, the gap between Jakovčević's enthusiasm and my restraint became clear and the conversation flagged. Jakovčević yawned. "I thought of Irma the other day, how she brought me a plush stuffed Alf from Germany," I said, trying to train my eyes on his broad, coarse fingernails and hairy chest that peered out from his undershirt, and not on the picture of my sister. He grew solemn. Why is it that people don't like to speak of their dead? Do they dump them in the ground and then forget about them? "American trash like Alf," he said, "that's how Satan finds us." "She gave one like it to Zoran." I wasn't giving up. I closed my eyes for a moment so I wouldn't see Irma come closer. "I'd love to see Zoran too," I went on, staring straight at Jakovčević's forehead as it grew sweatier. "How's he doing?" I finally managed to say. Jakovčević turned to look at his index fingers, which were circling one around the other. "Same old stuff," he said softly. Before I managed to ask anything more, he suddenly perked up, took my glass, and hopped over to the refrigerator. "I see you've finished your juice. Let me pour you some more," he said. Coming over with the brimming glass, he began talking about the nutritional benefits of wild blackberries, and as soon as I took the juice, he switched on the television. There was a television studio on the screen, with a moderator and a circle of six men in suits and ties. "Will you look at them," he said. "Communists, every last one of them." "And we who were dissidents back then, look at us," he added, and gestured in general to the room. I couldn't help but laugh at the word "dissidents." There he was, before my eyes, like he was then, newly a widower with a small child, who first set foot in our house on the island at some point in the late summer of 1990. Milka's relatives from K. sent him to see Irma. I'll never forget the moment he walked into the kitchen wearing a black satin shirt, leather pants, and patent leather shoes with heels, with a well-oiled mullet combed over his thinning scalp and a fluorescent watch on his wrist, holding little Đana in his arms and looking around the room in bewilderment, as if wondering, "And where do I put this?" Zoran and I burst out laughing. Irma struggled to stop laughing herself, and Mate looked him up and down seriously, with a little disgust, like he was an animal being seen for the first time. Only Milka strove to maintain an air of respect, so she sent Zoran and me out of the room. Did that first encounter determine his later unfortunate relationship with his stepson? I watched him now, while he tirelessly held forth about how Yugoslavia sabotaged his administration studies, and I wondered how to find a way to make him talk about Zoran. But before I could come up with something, a light rustling sound came from outside, the front door opened, and Anastazija stepped into the room. "Here's Staza back from work," said Jakovčević, as if speaking of a little child who'd successfully eaten lunch. I felt a sour mood come over me. Jakovčević always had to have a woman do the hard work of feeding him. No, he wasn't lazy, but he preferred expending his energy on his obsessions rather than on anything practical. Studying local history, an escargot farm, writing his memoirs, health juices, Jesus—all of these were ways of avoiding a proper confrontation with this house. Anastazija came over, proffered her hand, and, with a gentle smile, said, "We haven't seen each other for so long." We had only met a few times, but I always felt the very best of the available genetic material had come together in her. She was beautiful in a modest way, harmonious and moderate in every sense. The only disturbing thing about her was the utter lack of anything disturbing, though being disturbed is, indeed, in the eye of the beholder. A person with a restive spirit like mine had to wonder, while seeing the perfect balance between her black eyes, neither too mild nor too sharp, her regular yet soft facial features, her slender figure with no jutting bones or fuller curves, and her hair and skin, not too dark or too light, not too shiny or too dry: What could be hidden behind all that? Where was the point of vulnerability, an inadvertent gesture that might expose her month spent in a psychiatric ward a few years after her mother's death? It couldn't be found. Even her bangs hung there as if averse to making trouble, concealing the tension of the skull seen on every forehead, yet doing this translucently, with no animality in the growth of her hair, but with soft veils of locks casting her face with an additional gentility. She must have been very tired, but she kept her kindliness even when she apologized and went to her room to change. I wondered what time it was. If it were past nine, catching a bus to town would be a challenge. And where could I go then? Not back to Anica's. As if he were reading my thoughts, Jakovčević asked, "Staying at Anica's, Gorana?" I waffled for a second or two. "No," I said. "My visit was unplanned; I came on a project, and Anica happens to have guests. So, I figured I'd take a room at a hotel." When he chuckled, I felt relieved. "Dear Gorana," he said, overjoyed, "no, no. Why endure the fuss of a hotel? Stay here, there's all the room you could want. I'll make you eggs with chicory tomorrow morning, and then you can forge ahead to new victories." I breathed a sigh of relief, but for the sake of decency I pretended to feel uncomfortable—that I'd left my toothbrush in my suitcase at Anica's, that I had no vitamins or micellar cleansing water with me. "Well, if you insist," I said at last. "We're agreed," he said broadly, and went on conversing with the TV set. From that moment on, I could think of nothing but a comfortable bed and the bliss of a body that knows, as it lies down, that it will instantly drop off to sleep. Hold on a little longer, I bolstered myself, listening to the string of Jakovčević's fragmented and garbled political ideas. Anastazija came out of her room in a white cotton nightgown, took a pot from the refrigerator, and put it on the stove to warm up. "Would you like to eat, Gorana? Are you hungry?" asked Jakovčević. I wanted to say I wasn't, as one ought to in such circumstances, but hunger has its own way. The pasta with tomato sauce smelled more tempting than any food had smelled in my entire life. "I guess I could have a bite," I said offhandedly. Anastazija folded up the lace tablecloth and took the pot off the stove, while Jakovčević and I moved from the sofa to the table. "Staza's homemade pasta, none better," he said. He was right. I truly couldn't remember a dish that had made such an impression on me. The pliability of the fresh pasta offered comfort, yet it was just al dente enough to offer resistance to the teeth. Delicate, yet not flat. The sauce was simple yet not bland. Tart enough to entice, spicy enough to convince, but, above all, mellow to the point of flexibility, open for inscribing any number of meanings. A little olive oil, garlic, and basil, to ease interpretation. The dish gave the impression of a perfect equilibrium, like Anastazija. But people like me, Hladna, trust only their disquiet. After a gorgeous meal like this, I thought, something catastrophic must be heading my way. Behind my back, on the television, I heard the opening credits roll for the evening news. What, I thought, if they mention an apartment fire on Medveščak in Zagreb? Might the anchor say that an apartment has burned? That there are suspicions of malfeasance, and a search underway for the thirty-five-year-old architect who has been renting the apartment from a Zagreb homeowner? Gorana, Jakovčević might then ask, glancing at the TV over my shoulder, isn't your apartment in that part of town, hey, look, why, isn't that your building? I did my best to sit as tall as possible and engage his eyes as fixedly as I could with mine. Ah yes, the forces of evil, I agreed. Ah yes, former Communist cadres infiltrating all pores of life. Ah yes, the insidious decadence of gay men. He only nibbled at the pasta, because he'd eaten his evening meal earlier. "Come on," I said, plying him with more, infusing my offer with humor. "Have some more with us, don't be a party breaker, now." But while he devoted himself to chewing, I sensed that over the mouthfuls he was still listening to the TV news, and I was forced to say something like, "So what was it you were saying about Soros's secret plots?" I breathed a sigh of relief when the sports coverage began. Jakovčević, unfortunately, wasn't interested in sports, so he went on with new vigor to air his and others' crazy ideas. I clutched at the table edge. "Anastazija, need any help with the dishes?" I tried. "No need, thank you," she said. Why did she always have to be so polite? Again, a gap appeared in the conversation, and Jakovčević, slowly but steadily, overcame the mild dissatisfaction that had worn him down and confused him, perhaps because he couldn't precisely identify its origin. "We go to bed early here, Gorana," he said finally, his eyes swimming as he watched Anastazija, who, while wrapping up the last tasks of the day, was going from the bathroom to her room and back, "but feel free to keep watching TV if you like." "No need, my day was also long," I said sincerely. He was quiet, yawning and patting the remote control on the table. I noticed that the door to the bathroom was ajar and the light was on inside. "Guests go first," said Anastazija. Then she added, like the proprietor of a bed-and-breakfast, "A toothbrush, clean towel, nightgown, and underwear, everything is laid out on the washing machine. If you need anything more, I'm here." I don't know why I felt so awkward about going into their bathroom. Maybe I was afraid of leaving my bag behind, which I'd left on the sofa. Or it was the question of the room itself? Everyone, Hladna, is totally wrong who thinks of the table as the center of a house—there is no more intimate space than the bathroom. If a guest enters it, they'll discover the hidden side of their host. This bathroom was not dirty or messy, yet it was showing wear. The scaling that had built up over the years on the faucet grooves, the ribbed shower hose and the joints, naturally melted into the matte yellow-white tiles and walls, lending them an impression of both petrification and fragility. It smelled like a hospital—cheap bleach. My eyes stung from the neon light. I closed the door but didn't turn the key in the lock. I was afraid, how can I explain this, that the key might break in the lock and nobody would ever be able to get me out of there.

On the washing machine, next to the towel and toothbrushes, I recognized a fancy pink satin nightgown of Irma's that she'd bought in the 1980s in Germany, and lacy lilac panties with a high waist, which probably were Irma's as well. While I got undressed and stepped under the shower, I didn't have the feeling I was washing and seeing to the most ordinary daily routine, but that I was readying my body for a major and important change. From now on, I felt, I would have to let circumstances guide me the way patients do. I was too tired to go on clutching frantically at life. Let go, said the warm water to my body. Let go, Gorana, whispered the cocoa fragrance in the soapsuds. Suds yourself. Pat yourself dry. Put on your dead sister's panties. Wear her nightgown. Sleep in her house. I did everything obediently, but when I felt the lace scratchily wedge right on the joint between my thigh and my labia, and sensed the weak embrace of the satin—not cool, not warm—my nose identified Irma's fragrance, more from memory than reality, the fragrance of baby powder, and I felt like marching out, sitting Jakovčević and Anastazija down, and telling them all about my last two days. You may rightly assume, Hladna, that I did not. I pulled myself together and emerged clean and buoyant, and almost burst out laughing when I saw Jakovčević, who, with his big belly and chest hair, in white boxers, was sitting on the sofa, which had been opened up into a bed. "Do you mind sleeping with Staza in the double-decker? The bed in this room is busted," he said, directing me to the door of the little room where Zoran used to sleep. "No problem," I said. "Better than sharing the bed with you," I joked badly. He shot me such a sad and humiliated glance, I immediately regretted my quip. This was a man whose two wives had died, I scolded myself, who was probably looked down upon by the village, who basically cut his ties with his difficult family when he married Irma, a questionable woman with her questionable kid. He must have been terribly lonely. Anastazija opened the door to her room. "Come on in," she said and went off to the bathroom. I entered gingerly and drew the door partway closed behind me. The room was very small but surprisingly comfortable: shaggy yellow bedspreads on both beds, a lively desk to the right of the door, and a small, half-opened window on which the silvery curtains swayed, letting something inexplicable yet reliable into the room, a little like the barely audible stirring of the moonlit pine needles outside. The long wall behind the bed was painted with verdant floral scenes, calming at first glance, but at a second or third glance were full of hidden life, little sprites peering from behind the leaves and snails sliding along the stems, bees frozen in mid-flight and a monkey's eye that looked down from the ceiling. Every free centimeter of the walls was covered with shelves filled with more than just books. There were records and an occasional climbing vine. On one of the shelves, there was a nice wooden record player. On another, a straw hat. Many little odds and ends that couldn't be taken in all at once, but were delightful when discovered. The light of a simple copper ceiling lamp doubled the warmth of the yellow-orange beds, creating an atmosphere in which there was something old-fashioned yet also fresh. I lay on the lower bunk, on which the bedspread had been folded back, covered myself, and tried to read the titles of the books. Again, the disquiet in me. How was it possible for a room like this to be in such a house? Flowers don't grow among brambles. I heard Jakovčević and Anastazija exchanging a few quiet words through the partly closed door. She came into the room and closed the door partway again. I smiled. "Do you like to read?" I asked. "Of course, I studied literature," she said with her famous politeness. And then the impenetrable elegance with which she closed the window and climbed up onto the upper bunk. "Daddy," she called softly once she was up there. I saw his broad hand slip through the gap between the door and the doorframe and turn out the light. "Good night," he whispered. "Good night." "Good night." And night suddenly fell, heavy and clumsy. I felt Anastazija's breathing in the dark. I wanted to tell her she didn't have to live this way, that this house will inevitably turn her into something tough and self-satisfied, like weeds, but instead I whispered, "Anastazija, where is Zoran?" I felt her breathing stop. "On the island," she said. Her voice. This was the fissure I'd been waiting for. I can describe her voice in no other way than to say it was like freshly dug loam into which a heavy boot treads: on the surface mellow and relaxed, in texture soft and translucent, a dark, ripe color, while in its final uttered sound it abruptly sinks away, pressed into the very center of its pain. I knew what being "on the island" meant for Zoran. No, he was not in our house. He was at the psychiatric hospital that was two villages away from ours, on the shore of a sparsely settled, craggy cove. He'd already spent over a year there some eight or nine years before, and somehow everybody knew it was just a question of time before he'd return. On my back, I stared into the dark and thought about Zoran's life and all sorts of other things that elbowed their way into my head; I was too tired to impose any order on the chaos. I knew I should be thinking about my next move, but I didn't feel up to it. I could hear Jakovčević's blessed snoring from beyond the half-closed door; Anastazija pretended to be asleep. Night masterfully occupied the space, imbuing the house with a modicum of independence. The refrigerator got louder, the wood siding crackled, the little clock on Anastazija's desk ticktocked as if it were much bigger. The whine of a belated mosquito. The nearly silent brush of nocturnal breeze over the windowpane. Night: a time when we have a clearer sense of the miniature beings that live with us and on us. All those spiders drawing their strands of saliva over our furniture, the mites in the mattresses, and the bacteria in our guts. My second night free of bedbugs, I thought, not without a wistful twinge. I don't know, Hladna, why Sergej came to mind just then. Perhaps the sleepless night reminded me of the first night at the symposium, also sleepless. What had kept me awake then were the shiny, wine-red ribbons on the beige drapes in the hotel room and the reproduction of a picture by Ivan Generalić in a gilded plastic frame. Even in the dark I felt them there. All of this will one day be gone, I thought, this hotel full of architects will vanish into the viscous Zagorje mud, but this plasticized Generalić and the polyester drapes will outlive us all. I don't know why I remember feeling that the architects asleep in the other rooms were both kindred and foreign. At around 2 a.m. I went down to the first floor. This was a small family hotel in rural Zagorje and it didn't have a bar, but the girl at the front desk was so bored, she was glad to bring me a glass of red wine. I sat in the lobby, which looked like someone's living room: a lot of wood, brown leather, and a proper fireplace where a fire was still smoldering. Through the window by which I sat, I could see out across patches of snow from the week before to the shadow of a man, smoking. He did this slowly, easily, even though outside on that January night, it must have been very cold. When he finally came in, he didn't seem chilled to the bone, though aside from his dark jeans and shoes, all he was wearing was a thin, black sweater. He briefly rubbed his hands together, just for the sake of it, more as if he were brushing ash off of them than warming them up, then immediately sat down in the armchair across from me, next to the fireplace. "A hotel for non-smokers," he said with a barely visible scoff, "yet no balconies." He said this as if we'd already been talking earlier about the hotel's drawbacks. I didn't answer. I watched him take the poker, and, lounging comfortably in the armchair, his legs crossed, he poked with relaxed curiosity at the glowing remains of the embers. Right away, I took to his style. He looked like an aristocrat, a maniac, and a monk. While he stared into the fire, dressed in black, his arms sticking out like the pale, wiry limbs of some underground creature, his graying hair combed back, and with dark circles under his eyes, he gave the impression of a person who had barely survived lengthy torment, and now, with a dedicated nihilism, he was staring at this tiny source of light he'd been given, unexpectedly, as a gift. When he turned his gaze to me, his aquamarine eyes produced such a contrast to the space around him, everything he said sounded credible. "Now that Crta, he's quite the nasty piece of work," he said, as if we'd already been talking about Crta, and then he went on to talk about his past with Crta when they were punk rockers, without any sense of trying to impress me, but as if we were an elderly married couple who already understood each other perfectly. I managed to figure out that the person nicknamed Crta was actually Sreten Jokić, the informal boss of the Belgrade architectural "team," and the man sitting in front of me was the driver of the van that had brought the "team" to Zagorje. I noticed his pointy shoes of gray-black snakeskin, which, though a little old-fashioned and, actually, ugly, lent his overall appearance something timeless, and if, while speaking, he were to look up at the ceiling, the tattoo peeking from his collar—the tips of some sort of tails or arms—would give the impression he was plucking himself, without despair but with persistence, from the darkness of his clothing, from the wood-and-leather lobby, and from his entire life. He gossiped about the architects, coldly but with no malice, as if it were his duty to inform me about their bad habits: Knežević had a temper, Novaković irritated all of them, Aleksić was secretly farting the whole way in the van. I took up the gauntlet: Šantek likes to boast, Zrnčić is clueless, Kurelt hires his lovers. Ćolak, Bilić, Stanišić, Vidak, Majer, Radulović, Robović, Car—there were so many of them, and each had flaws enough for a very long conversation. At about five we said our goodbyes to each other and to the woman at the front desk, and then each of us went to our room. The next night I didn't even try to fall asleep. After midnight I went down, without the slightest bit of excitement, knowing I'd find him in the same place. That was the first night we spent together in a hotel bed. The next four were much like the first, so much so that now, lying in Jakovčević's house, I had to count on my fingers how many nights there had been, because in my memory they seemed to go on and on. Those nights, ordinary to the point of coldness, yet so unreal: always in his room, where there was no Generalić on the wall or ribbons in the drapes, and the morning view of the hills from the third floor provided more impetus for surviving the day. By day we didn't see each other, only once or twice in passing, from a distance. Though for me all this was new and unusual and ultimately led me to marry a stranger, I can't recall feeling any disquiet. I remembered, and now I also remember, that it felt more like the end of something rather than a beginning. As if I were bringing to a close something that had been inscribed long before. After the next to last night, early on the morning of the thirtieth, I called someone I'd known well in my student days who worked at the office of the justice of the peace, and after long, haggling negotiations I managed to arrange for us to be married the very next day. On the thirty-first, early in the morning, we got into the van and drove to Zagreb, and before the workday started we were married, using black plastic rings from Kinder eggs, which had been left in my purse ever since Igor's two-year-old twins visited our office. Our witnesses were two cleaning ladies. I remember us amicably joshing around with big-eared Mislav, our connection at the office of the justice of the peace, who was so thrown off by this breach of protocol that he kept dropping his pen and fumbling with the papers, and he checked Sergej's Croatian documents over and over, almost as if he couldn't quite believe such a person had been born in his country. We returned to Zagorje in time for me to take part in the closing of the symposium. The closing speeches were held at the local Cultural Center, as the rest of the gathering had been. The small hall had a stage that was a bit too high, so the audience suffered from aching necks. I remember listening to old Joško Dulčić's speech, and I couldn't understand a word he said. All I did was watch his wobbly jaw, from which the words tumbled as if from a broken machine. From time to time he'd stop, and, with his mouth slack, he'd stare out at the back of the room as if someone had entered the hall whom he recognized, but he couldn't recall their name. Then from the corners of his mouth would drip a shiny stream of saliva, and his eyes would float glumly into his cataracts. Why was it, then, that he looked over at me and smiled? Elena Sajko was sitting, gray-haired and colorful, on the chair to the left. I was horrified by the moment when we would all rise to leave the hall and Elena would take me by the arm, pat me maternally, and explain to the elderly architects that I was the best thing that had happened to her since the late 1980s and the Triangle project. She would be as she was: frank, dignified, capable of nonviolently foisting herself on everybody, turning her diminutive stature into a sort of kindly rebuke, so people wouldn't feel bad about being so tall, round, and warm. But only I would be able, with my arm, to feel the full weight of her intelligence that had been left untapped, contained inside her body from the very start and finally trapped in it in the 1990s—a weight so physical that it ultimately destroyed her right leg. How, I thought, will I usher her out of the hall, limping as she was and nearly paralyzed? I felt the urge to pee. I got up. I remember Elena shooting me a questioning look. I remember Igor waving from the other side of the hall. He probably wanted to remind me that later we'd be closing the gathering. "I'm just going to the restroom," I whispered to Elena and slipped out quickly. The restroom was next to the front entrance. It was narrow and old, with a shit-smeared toilet seat in the first stall and a water tank high on the wall that had no pull string in the second. I went into the second, covered the seat with toilet paper, sat, and peed. That's that, I thought. That's that. Someone entered the first stall. Familiar-sounding steps, then the sharp sound of urine breaking the surface of the water from high above. Sergej. When he finished, he washed his hands, but even though he was silent, I knew he hadn't left. I peeked under the partition. Yes, the snakeskin shoes were waiting for me to come out. I don't know how long I sat inside, but when I finally did come out, he was still there, leaning on the wall, his arms crossed, calm. Only his believable eyes followed me while I went over to the faucet. "We have to leave immediately. The van is waiting for us at the entrance," I heard him say from behind me. I didn't ask where we were going. I wiped my hands on the paper towel that was next to the faucet, getting goose bumps from the newsprint-like texture. Enthusiastic applause could be heard from the hall. "We need to go to the hotel and pick up our things." Our eyes met. He nodded. This simple nod established a sort of dark alliance between us. All that we later did was merely a logical continuation of our eyes meeting and his affirming nod. Instead of attending the final lunch with the architects, I went off with Sergej to the hotel, packed up, checked out, and then sat on the passenger seat in the van and let him take me wherever he wanted. I felt a powerful sense of relief, but I couldn't tell you, Hladna, where it had sprung from. Why had I suddenly begun to feel physical aversion to the company of other architects? I don't know. I only know that the aversion was so powerful that I was prepared to marry a stranger and abandon everything. We set off for Belgrade. Never had the rutty village roads seemed so capacious. At first there was a lingering fear the police might come after us, but over the phone Sergej managed to persuade Crta, on the strength of their shared punk rock history, to let him leave. I wrote to Igor that I'd be taking a brief vacation and turned off my phone. You are probably wondering how we managed to stretch the trip from Zagorje to the border with Serbia to sixteen days. Because, as I now recalled, sliding back and forth in Irma's nightgown between sleep and wakefulness, we set off on January 31 and returned to Zagreb on February 15. Sixteen unreal days. What did we do? After we passed through Zaprešić, where I could break my term deposit and withdraw my savings, we circumvented Zagreb and went off the highway near Ivanić-Grad, where we enjoyed a peaceful afternoon and slept over in a hotel. The next day, we took smaller local roads that ran parallel to the highway. I remember the trip as a sort of horizontal free fall. Sergej's life suddenly appeared like a rolling globe. I was holding on to it, and it demolished everything standing before me—all the villages and towns off the beaten path along the Sava River Valley—freeing me of the need to be an architect, to be constantly thinking about possibilities for saving the built environment, leaving only devastation behind us under the snow. The route we took followed the stages of his life story. As we drove through Novoselec, he was an only child, his father an officer of the Yugoslav People's Army, a war orphan, and his mother, a teacher from a bourgeois Zagreb family; he spent his early childhood as a denizen of Pula; from the age of six he was a Belgrader; by the time we drove through Popovača, he'd reached the age of eleven, the war came, and his father left the armed forces and struggled with depression; as we pulled into Voloder, Sergej was already furious at his father for being such an introvert and drinking in secret; by Repušnica, he didn't know what he wanted from life—he vandalized kiosks and joined his first punk band; in Kutina, he'd settled on the study of theology, and this nearly did in his father; by Lipovljani, his father did, indeed, die, as Sergej was completing his studies, and now he didn't know what to do with theology, as it was no longer of any use to him; by Novska, he'd begun to paint, always in black-and-white but with boundless energy; in the vicinity of Rajić, he spent a year living with his mother in Belgrade, working at a warehouse; by Okučani, he took off for the Netherlands to look for freedom; the whole way to Gradiška, he made it no farther than a flower nursery, where he eked out his living earning minimum wage; by Cernik, he suddenly picked up and left for Paris; by Rešetar, he tried to break into the Paris art scene and made love to a young blonde Parisian woman with squirrel-like teeth, but even by Staro Petrovo Selo, he hadn't managed to pull free of jobs like pizza delivery man or cab driver; by Orlovac, discouraged, he returned to Belgrade and his mother and spent half a year in a depression much like the Slavonian barrens; by the time we reached Sibinj, he'd rejoined one of his old bands, was reading a lot, and lived on his mother's salary all the way to Velika Kopanica, when his mother came down with breast cancer, retired, and found him a job at her old school as a janitor; by Babina Greda, he'd fucked a redheaded teacher, the principal's wife, in the teachers' lounge, so his mother gave him some of her savings and sent him off on a trip; by Privlaka, he continued wandering the world, through North America, South America, Africa, and Asia, supporting himself with odd jobs, on all possible drugs and in fleeting love affairs; by Otok, he was apprehended at the Australian border with a banned seed he'd brought from Indonesia. The situation was becoming complicated. At this point, he was tired of so much excitement, so by Đeletovci he returned to Belgrade and his mother, tried to rise again on the punk scene with his own band, and drove a cab; by Tovarnik, he was painting again, always in black-and-white but with boundless energy—he also worked as a bus driver and a private driver working off the books; by Šarengrad, he'd met me, and that was when we were pulling into Ilok. I wrote, Hladna, that ex-punk rockers are the worst. But Sergej wasn't ex, no, Sergej demolished villages and towns in that aristocratic-maniacal-monkish way of his, calmly and coldly, his legs crossed, spinning the globe with one finger, turning it with such speed that, with my model life as a woman who was stubbornly ascending the architectural Everest, I was barely able to hold on. The fall was long, because I fell from a very great height. Still, I can't remember ever being afraid. All I felt was a sort of melancholic curiosity: What's next? Where is this all going? I can't fully explain to you how we managed to spend most of my savings in a mere sixteen days. True, we stayed at the most expensive village accommodations we could find, ordered the most expensive lunches and dinners and then changed our minds and ordered something else, drank the most expensive wines, visited every local adrenaline park, ordered mountain-climbing equipment so we could climb Psunj, paid for rounds of drinks for everyone in every village tavern, made gifts to the association for the protection of hares and Slavonian embroidery, culture and art societies and minority associations, donated funds for the renovation of monuments and new windows for a regional school, visited doleful village casinos and clubs with middle-aged singers in sequined outfits who had carrot-like complexions or morose strippers with varicose veins, but, again, I was half asleep while keeping count. This must have come to a sum greater than 180,000 kunas. My brain, defeated by the figure, tried to remember each individual outlay, but my body was too tired. Sleep, sleep, sleep, it whispered, preventing me from keeping track. But then my brain threw ropes with little hooks on them over my skin and painfully dragged my body from sleep, hissing, Count, you must know each and every, even the tiniest, detail, if you want to grasp how the crash happened. So, I counted, but I could not reach any conclusion. But one moment kept appearing before my eyes: the moment when we arrived at the border between Croatia and Serbia. February 15. A mild, clear day, a bit like early spring. We slept at a little wooded estate in the foothills of Fruška Gora. Eggs and bacon for breakfast, the smell of wet branches and spring grass. The minuscule anxiety of chickens. Around noon we set off for Ilok. I remember the saleslady at the gas station, a large woman who kept awkwardly maneuvering with her belly, as if she were wearing a swimming ring. She kept bumping into things. She felt compelled to ask where we were coming from and where we were going, why not buy a few Bounties with two Twixes, how long Sergej had been smoking Marlboros, and would we be drinking beer while we're driving, and then she stabbed her sharp gray eyes into our faces in such a way that

I couldn't shake them off long after we'd pulled out of the gas station. She looked as if we were harming her by leaving. I was only able to chase her from my thoughts after we crossed the Croatian border. But Sergej's mother occurred to me while we were in the transit area. Soon we'll cross into Serbia, I thought, we'll arrive in Belgrade in the afternoon, and she'll be waiting for us in her shabby apartment with a roasted chicken on the table. She'll be overjoyed to see us; she'll create an agreeable atmosphere in which the aromas of ajvar and fresh bread will mingle; there will be clean napkins and potatoes roasted in fat. She'll be sitting there—surrounded by the books she'd read and the crossword puzzles she'd solved, the priceless mementos in the glass display cases—an elderly lady who still kept herself up, so real, with her aching hips and the lipstick that got into the wrinkles around her lips. How will Sergej, I thought—when his mother kisses him and he blushes and quickly wipes his cheek, when he inadvertently smiles at the smell of the familiar roast, when he sits back in the armchair shaped long ago by his back—how will he ever be able to be the same man I met in the lobby of the hotel? He will no longer be capable of demolishing villages and cities, and he won't show any interest in ruining his familial apartment, the building it was in, and the street. An environment, irreparable and unmasterable, completely unknown, will surround me on all sides. I felt myself breathing with difficulty. The sun filled the van and awakened the smell of plastic and sweat long preserved in the cracks of the seat. I remember how my heart began to pound more vigorously as we slowly approached the mustachioed customs officer, and when he looked at us from under his dark, bushy eyebrows and asked for our passports, I couldn't move. "Gorana, passports," said Sergej. "Excuse me?" I whispered, not moving. "Passports," he said a little nervously, then took my purse from me, rummaged around in it, and handed the customs officer, who was already becoming suspicious, our documents. "Sergej," I managed to utter, "I want to go back." He looked at me with cold incredulity. "Back?" "I can't do this, I must go back to Zagreb, I'm not well." "She must go to Zagreb," he said to himself. "Yes," I agreed, timidly, "I must go back. I've used up all my meds." Then I took a minute to come up with a viable ailment. "I have a disorder. Autoimmune," I added, not without malicious relish. It's an amusing fact that people usually don't ask anything when you say you have an autoimmune disorder, right, Hladna? He shot me a doubting look, and then, disappointed but conciliatory, he said, "Okay, we'll turn around after we enter Serbia." And so we did. We drove for a kilometer or two, turned around, crossed the border again, and, without stopping, headed for Zagreb. We arrived at Medveščak in the late afternoon. We spent the next three days in my apartment, going out only for food, drink, and cigarettes. The eighteenth was his thirty-ninth birthday. I bought a chocolate torte and a bottle of cognac, and it was good in an empty, mechanical sort of way. I generally had two contradictory feelings during those days: my apartment began to feel, with Sergej's presence, like a new and interesting place, but the fact that I was no longer in charge of my own space filled me with distress. I couldn't find my way to my sheets, my couch, my refrigerator, my table, or my bathroom, which he clogged with wet towels and alien hair. He was always sitting or lounging somewhere, wearing my cactus pajamas, firmly anchored in his body, which did not show the slightest intention of disappearing. I realized now that I had a husband. He digested food at my table, he climaxed inside me, he lounged in my beautiful ivory-hued armchair. When, at dusk on the eighteenth, Jere called with the news of Milka being on her deathbed and said that I had to come if I wanted to say goodbye, I didn't want Sergej to come with me. Not because I would have been ashamed of our hasty wedding, but because I knew his presence would prevent me from my intention of truly engaging with my mother for the last time. But he insisted on driving me down there in the van. He insisted on being my husband. At early dawn on February 19, we set off from Zagreb. A kilometer or so beyond Plitvice, we stopped at a gas station. I tossed the panties I hadn't remembered to change during my sleepless night into the wastebasket in the bathroom. I bought a bag of mixed nuts. Soon we turned off the highway onto the old road at my behest, although now, lying on the lower bunk beneath Anastazija, who had fallen soundly asleep, I couldn't remember what it was I had been searching for. I remembered that in Sergej's gaze, and in the way he agreed to turn off the highway, I saw the dark understanding I'd first observed in the bathroom in Zagorje, but I couldn't grasp more than that. Panties, snacks, the dark, the hospital. Only that. I slid around in Irma's nightgown from sleep to waking and back. Remember, said my mind, remember those five minutes before the crash that are, for you, in the dark. The brain strained to recognize the logic in the bag of mixed nuts, the chaos of hazelnuts, walnuts, Brazil nuts, cashews, almonds, peanuts, and pistachios; it strained to reconstruct each movement, each thought before the fateful turn, but my body was overtired. At one moment longed-for sleep, ugly and heavy, took over. I dreamed of Igor. I tried to go over to him, longing for him to hug me, but when he finally agreed to, it was as if I were in someone else's arms—Anica's, Kiddo's, Milka's, Jakovčević's, or Sergej's. I woke before dawn. The first light already lent contours to everything in the room, but things still had a dark face, deep in their own simple materiality, and nothing was watching me. I had to get out of there—this was my first thought. I snuck out of bed without a sound, let Irma's nightgown slip from me, and pulled on my dress, which was there waiting for me at the foot of the bed. For a few minutes I wavered and then put on Anastazija's white canvas sneakers, leaving the ballet flats behind. On my tiptoes, holding my last pair of dirty panties in my hand, I went out into the living room. Jakovčević was on his back, his belly bare, sucking in air as if filling a bellows and then expelling it with a hiss. My purse sat on the floor by the couch. I took it, stuffed my panties in, kept a cautious eye on Jakovčević to be sure he was sleeping, then very slowly, making the least noise possible, opened the front door, and out I went. Dawn. How can a person not love it, Hladna, my dear? Dawn isn't morning, such an untidy time, passed over in one's search for the identity of a day. No, dawn is a privileged moment for emerging from nonexistence. Rising from the dead. A time when it is possible, with your back to the dark from which you've come, to observe the day awaiting you without fear, with good excitement, like something small and powerless that needs your help for it to be defined. Dawn. Everything is already there, but not yet weighed down by a name of its own. The birds don't bother anybody. An ordinary road meanders among ordinary pine trees to a small town where streetlamps, forgotten, are still lit. On the seashore only pansies, boxwood bushes, and holly oak trees. A sea with no threat. Calm as it rocks the boats and savors the mellow beauty. The sky clear, free of the tyranny of the sun. The buses still not on the road. I turned toward town, enjoying the ease with which the space allowed itself to be traversed. My muscles and bones ached, but I felt fresh. Here and there somebody would come out on a balcony, stretch, and watch me with curiosity, the aromas of coffee and butter on toast, here and there an older man swimming out into the open sea. I reached town hardly noticed at all. Calmly, I boarded an empty bus at the terminal and took it to the ferry port. Knowing that I might have a few small coins left, I rummaged through every pocket in my purse and did, indeed, manage to collect nine kunas. Those, with the six kunas and twenty lipas still in my wallet, should do. You can imagine, then, the unpleasant surprise when the woman at the ticket counter handed me my ticket and said, "Eighteen kunas, please." I'd forgotten the high-season rates were still in effect until the beginning of October, and that day was the twenty-somethingth or thirtieth of September. This set me back and I automatically began digging through my purse, though I knew there would be nothing there to find. Two kunas and eighty lipas—this was all that stood between me and the island. I turned to look around, seeking help. The man in line behind me began testily shuffling his feet. The light-colored linoleum on the floor, still clean, shone coldly. I mumbled an indistinct apology and walked away. The ferry was waiting at the terminal, open and nearly empty. I went over. At the entrance, by the ramp, I spotted Tomislav, a friend from childhood. He was standing there, suntanned and stout, a little proud and a little shy, like a schoolkid who, for the first time, puts on a clean white shirt and pants ironed with a crease. "Hey, Tome," I called. He didn't hear me. "Tome!" I said again, louder this time. He looked over, friendly and inquisitive, but without recognition. I came closer. "Gorana," he blurted with his good old broad and noisy affect. "Well, will you have a look at her," he said with a heartfelt smile. "You used to be blonde." I remembered he'd had a crush on me when we were kids. "You won't believe what happened to me," I said. "I left my wallet at Anica's, so I can't pay for my ticket, but I need to get to the island. I have to find some of Milka's papers that are still there." I was about to embroider further on my story to make it sound more credible, but he interrupted, laid his hands on my shoulders, and said in a low voice, "Of course I'll let you on. Just stand right here with me until I wrap up things. You never know who's watching, right?" I almost burst out laughing when he winked. He cranked his voice up to its usual, island pitch and began calling out to the few passengers standing nearby. Meanwhile he told me all about his ten-year-old son's doltish teacher, about the unrecognized vocal talent of his seven-year-old daughter, about his wife's tyrannical boss, about his crazy mother and even crazier father, about "all of them who screw him over at work." He spoke with no bitterness, but with a certain naive indignation, which tickled me. When he'd finished boarding the passengers and raised the ramp, he took me to the captain's cabin. "Here's one of our very own. She's working wonders up in the metropolis," he introduced me to the crew. The boys were tanned and loud and laughed in a way that gave the impression they had incredibly white teeth, even though they didn't. Each of them competed to be the first to show me what each button was for. The captain, an older man from the city, eyed me without excitement but with a friendly, paternal interest. It was nice to finally relax a little while inspecting all the unfamiliar devices, screens, and numbers, following the sure hands that were repeating well-learned everyday routines. They chatted with me in dialect, imposing no distance, almost the way they talked among themselves but with more respect. Each found a connection to me, but these ties couldn't usurp the mood. They came from the realm of familial ties, friends of friends and very old island anecdotes, and they didn't make me anxious. Tomislav remembered me as a smart, pretty girl, a loyal friend, someone who courageously defended my convictions. Good old Tome. He so sincerely believed in the image of me he held in his mind that I, too, briefly believed it. There I was—attractive, smart, faithful, brave—standing atop the ferry and parting the seas to locate documents for my dying mother. Embracing fallacies about oneself is always the easiest, right? For the half hour that the ferry ride took, I relished the sense of direction, but, ultimately, we'd have to land, and I knew I'd be forced to choose whether to board the bus for our village or the one for Zoran's hospital. These were in two different directions, and my anxiety returned. With a weight on my chest, I said goodbye to Tome and the rest of the cheery crew and boarded the first bus that pulled up. You won't be surprised when I say it was the bus to Zoran. What was I hoping to accomplish with this visit? Surely, I didn't expect to pull him out of a state institution. So, what was I up to? Obtaining information that might help me?

Or only wrapping up my story, exhausting every last possibility for saving myself? I got off at the stop but didn't go any farther. I sat on a bench. It was about nine o'clock in the morning, and the sun was still mild. Filtering through the branches of a pine tree, which arched over the bus-stop shelter to my left, it gently compelled me to look either at the road down which the bus was disappearing into the woods or at the hospital across the cove. A dilapidated building, mundane, dirty white, bars on the windows. Nothing moved. Not a breath of wind, the sea like a mirror. The birds waiting for me to move. I pictured myself getting up, walking along the side path to the guard's little hut. The guard, a gray fellow with gray hair, moored on his heavy feet, would watch me with slow bewilderment. He'd know nothing about whether I could or could not enter; he'd call his boss. Glumly, he'd pick up the phone and explain my case. A gray woman, her hair coiffed in a sharp gray bob, would come striding out. Who am I, and do I know that these are not visiting hours? Gorana Hrabrov, I'd reply, with a PhD in architecture, recently arrived from Sweden, the United States, Addis Ababa, Mars, and within five minutes I must be off on my way to Lebanon, Peking, Thailand, Saturn, and I haven't seen my beloved nephew Zoran, with whom I grew up on this very island, for at least two years, or three—or is it ten? I'd hardly be able to contain myself while waiting for the moment when her bob would soften, when she'd smooth her skirt and say, "Oh, well, I guess we can make an exception." But what was it going to be like to go to Zoran, toting all these lies on my back? For though Zoran was the stupidest of all my nephews, he was the only one who understood people. This was the source of his misfortune. People said, "Irma has made such huge sacrifices as a mother." He knew they were really saying, "She made her bed and now she has to lie in it." People said, "He's not a bad guy, this Jakovčević." But he knew they were really saying, "Jakovčević got what was coming to him." I couldn't bear the thought of having to face his sad, piercing eyes. They were the same family eyes—Mate's—but in Zoran's case, tiny and black like peppercorns; they emphasized the naked fleshiness of his big ears, light curly hair, plump pink lips, and broad nose, and they turned the burliness of his bearing into weakness. Only the staunchly bristlelike hair along his low hairline saved him from sinking into total vulnerability. I pictured myself sitting across from him, separated only by a table that would seem tiny next to him, and when the warden with her bob haircut said, "Look who's come to see you, your young aunt from Sweden, the US, Addis Ababa, Mars," Zorko would look at me and instantly know I'd set fire to my apartment. How could I wound him like that, I, the last illusion he still cherished? I sat on the bench at the bus stop, motionless. Now and then a car drove by. The driver and passengers would glance briefly at me as they passed, and again the blue-green silence would settle over me. I thought about Zoran's life. I had memories of him from when he was seven or eight, when he had already acquired the bumbling clumsiness of a child who feels he shouldn't be as big as he was, a constant apology in posture and gesture that would culminate in rage. He seemed both slow-witted and wise. Our shared island childhood was guided by four parents: Milka, Mate, Kiddo, and Irma's voice over the phone. Kiddo, though only four years older than Zorko and eight years older than me, had always behaved as if he were our second dad. Zorko accepted this with his usual opaque impassivity, tough the way a brick is tough. Like a brick, he might have seemed capable of deflecting the rain, sun, or wind, but he lacked the internal flexibility to protect himself; instead he stood there, frozen, watching as, over time, the wear from the weathering reached a point where something big and powerful would come barreling through, a biblical storm or earthquake that would expose his masked fragility. That was Zorko. He put up with Kiddo ordering him around, with Milka's awful tenderness, as if she were kindly forgiving him for being who he was, with the moments of anger when Mate addressed him as "hey there, Mr. Padovan," as if Zoran were an outsider foisting himself on Mate's life, with the village keeping track of his every flaw, with his mother dumping him on the island so she could guard her peace with Jakovčević. But in the second half of the '90s, Zoran was buffeted by postwar horrors and hormonal tempests, and these proved to be too much for him. He enrolled in a trade school for butchers and developed a floundering, bearlike hostility. He came to the island less and less often. In his stead came news about him fighting and stealing, hanging out with kids I didn't want anywhere near me, and failing class after class at school. It all culminated in 1999, a little before Mate died, when Zoran ended up in jail. Later, he tried to pull himself together. He managed to graduate from night school but found holding down a job difficult. He'd always come up with some brutal truth about his boss in his clumsy, dark way that horrified people. He spent a little time with his mother and stepfather, a little at his father's place, and a little who knows where. It might have been around 2010 when he first ended up in the psychiatric ward. A few months later he heard Irma was sick. When he came back to K., after a year or so, he was quieter. He helped his mother and tried to get along with Jakovčević. He did his level best, and it seemed as if his maturity might save him. But then after Irma's death he fell apart again. He lived a little at his stepfather's, a little at his half sister Đana's, a little at his father's, but mostly who knows where. Now, with each memory he was growing bigger in my thoughts. I had the feeling I could spot one of his eyes behind the window bars of the hospital, black against a black background, an eye recognizable only by the particular restlessness that always comes to the surface from within such places. If I went in, I knew Zorko would grow to such a huge size, the warden and staff and guards and other patients would all disappear beneath him. There'd be nowhere for me to look away. I'll have to look him straight in the eyes. I'll have to witness the moment, in living Technicolor, when his still-surviving assumption of me as someone precious who'd been entrusted to him, clumsy as he was, would sink below the surface of those eyes as if into pools of oil. "Do you know, Goga, why it is I didn't go to school to train as a florist but as a butcher?" he'd ask me darkly. "I loved flowers, but I knew they can't be trusted." I couldn't bear the thought of him saying that, Hladna. I got up and strode down the road toward the woods, without knowing where I was going, but moving along fast enough to give the impression I was leaving the hospital behind me in every possible way. The road ran uphill in a northwesterly direction, veering westward after a time, passing mainly through uninhabited stretches of land overgrown with scrub pine or maquis. I skirted two villages, unnoticed. I walked along in Anastazija's comfortable sneakers, some of the time in the agreeably warm sun, some of the time in the agreeably cool shade. Perhaps even you, a city woman, will understand me when I say that an island has the power to keep a person intact while they think of themselves, meanwhile shedding the continental burden of their existence. Some may call this freedom, but I think of it as a specific kind of forgetting, visited upon us by the finite nature of our space. Regardless of the direction in which you look, the end is always close at hand, always a presence; the sea clearly holds the advantage, and the surroundings are not burdened by the endless possibilities of shaping that the mainland seems to offer in all four cardinal directions. Though an island can also be shaped, arranged, and devastated, interventions into it are less serious, sometimes even ridiculous, because nothing can truly touch its finality. An island is about forgetting the future. On it, a person feels they're more lucid than ever, yet they cannot take themselves altogether seriously. While I was walking toward the village where I'd spent my childhood, everything—my life, my career, the car crash, setting fire to my apartment—began feeling a little silly. Through my mind went the thoughts: I should be worried, there is no way out, at any moment the police might find me. I should have been worried, but I was no longer able to muster even the most ordinary twinge of anxiety. On an island, a pine tree is a pine tree, lavender is lavender, a woman walking is a woman walking. The sun is stronger, the insects are doing their simple jobs. A logical tiredness entered my feet. The first few houses appeared as I came down into the village, and then there were more. The road widened. In the yards, though mostly empty, there was the feel of a festive atmosphere. White tablecloths were spread here and there on tables, tastefully set with dishes and silverware, and bottles of wine and pitchers of water glistening in the shade, waiting on the patios. Here and there, through balcony doors and windows, could be heard a wooden spoon knocking the rim of a cooking pot, a cleaver chopping meat, or someone sipping hot soup to taste it for salt. Aromas wafted by of sauces and roasted lamb, freshly sliced bread, vinegar nipping at lettuce. The reality reached me from afar, with a delay, but it didn't take me long to remember—this was all about the day dedicated to St. Mihovil, whom the village had embraced as its patron saint. I left the road running along the shore to the ferry port, and from there I turned left onto the sandy stretch of the waterfront, finding myself abruptly in the middle of the old village center, at the heart of the festivities. The Mass had just ended, and a river of people was pouring out from the square in front of the church: men wearing shirts so tight, they needed extra room around them so they could swing their arms as they walked, as if they were rowing; women teetering around in high heels over the bumpy cobblestones; little girls dressed as if for their weddings, encased in foamlike tulle, the fragile beauty of which always had to be kept level; little boys in ties who scampered around underfoot; old folks who were proudly and peacefully brandishing their big bellies, and old folks without bellies who had to talk a lot in order to earn their space; teenagers clutching their phones; a few clusters of widows, black, dry, and crackling; loners who took the first opportunity to step away from the mainstream and disappear down side streets. Pastel colors, hair spray, pungent perfumes. All the people looked familiar to me; parts of their faces, their movements, postures, gestures, and grimaces, and their voices and laughter summoned fragments of memory that buried me on all sides, but there was no way I could bind the fragments into a whole that would be coherent enough for me to actually recognize any of them. And they, too, noticed me and nodded without a sound, as if they knew who I was but couldn't place the name and couldn't call out to me. I easily could have avoided their gazes—I knew every alleyway in the village, and finding a shortcut to our house would have been simple. But for some reason I made no effort to hide. Actually, I think I wanted the village to recognize me, because hiding had become too onerous. Did you know, Hladna, that telling lies isolates you more than disease or death? I approached the small square in front of the church, where a very long table had been set up. People were still leaving the church, but the numbers were dwindling. Families with children lingered briefly by two stands selling gummy candy, trinkets with flashing lights, plastic saints, and water pistols or by the popcorn machine and ice cream freezer, but soon they went on their way, hurrying home to eat. At the table, which shone with a dark whiteness under umbrellas, several people were already taking their seats. This wasn't a public free-for-all, after which the priest or head of the municipality would be doling out fried sardines or calamari. No, this table had been festively set, with double plates, tall glasses, and an arrangement of red roses and sequined butterflies in the middle. I saw Zvjezdana Jureško, who—after coming out of her stone house on the edge of the square where the waterfront continued, separated from the church by only a narrow little street—placed two bowls of salad greens on the table. I definitely wanted to avoid her, but before I managed to adjust my trajectory across the square enough to the left to dip into a side street and slip behind the church, she spotted me and started calling me loudly by name, waving energetically and a little angrily, as if she'd been waiting for me all morning, and here I was, showing up only now. I went over. "Where have you been, Little Miss Hrabrov, fuck it all," she said too loudly, only slightly softening the sharp lines of her face. All the heads shot up and watched me in silence. "Have a seat, the meat is coming," she said, as if my place at the table had been waiting for me all this time. There are people like that, who are appalled by the horrific weight of their military character, but they are able to bend reality to their will to such a degree that a person instantly feels safe with them, even though having grasped the fake nature of that sense of safety. Zvijezda will look after you, ran through my head, not without irony, all you need to do is sit and wait. I took the last chair in the row, across from an old man wearing a dark-blue beret whom I recognized as Zvjezdana's father, known in the village by the nickname Vlajo, ever since he had moved to the island with his wife and three children from a backwoods place on the mainland to work at the fish-processing plant. He watched me with a stony gaze while I drank glass after glass of water, but didn't say a word. The conversation at the table grew more animated, and nobody paid attention to me anymore. From the spot where I was sitting, through the open door of the house, I could see how Zvjezdana and two girls I didn't know were arranging lamb on platters. Zvjezdana's husband, looking like a teenager who'd grown up too fast, flew from kitchen to table and back, bringing drinks, bread, toothpicks, the napkins they'd forgotten. I couldn't name most of the guests. In the row on my side of the table I didn't recognize anybody, and across from me, aside from Zvjezdana's father, I recognized her gloomy brother and slow sister—someone who had always looked as if she were an elderly woman investing a lot of effort in keeping up appearances. Next to her sister sat a ruddy man. I vaguely remembered that he was her sister's husband from Slavonia, and some of the younger guests might have been their sons or daughters, whom I also remembered only vaguely as children. From the church emerged the last of the congregation, skinny women in modest skirts and white shirts who had stayed behind after the Mass to contribute to the collection plate, and the singers from the choir who radiated the artificial joy that people of the church recognizably possess. Quiet Uncle Ante, who always collected the alms and, generally, was "with the priest," was the last to come out. He briefly raised his arms to greet everyone at the table and then plodded down the square to his house. Shortly after that, the priest himself appeared, locked the church door, and took the seat at the head of the table. He was a new priest whom I hadn't met, very young, pale and thin, handsome in a lifeless sort of way, like a sacred image, and so serious that the noise around the table abruptly hushed with his arrival. Zvjezdana and the girls brought out the platters of meat, and then the typical fierce chewing and gulping—more like an athletic discipline than a feast—could begin. To my left sat two teenage boys, Zvjezdana's sons—I remembered—and to the right, at the other head of the table, sat Zvjezdana. How can I describe her to you, Hladna, without facing you with an improbable character? Real courage is needed, I admit, for a person to encounter her suddenly, face-to-face, so perhaps it's better for you to see her the way I saw her then, in profile. Though sitting there, bolt upright in that familiar combative way of hers, indicating she was poised to eat the entire table and all the guests, she nevertheless used a fork and knife for the meat, and was only a little greasy around her only slightly smeared, bright-red lipstick. Her platinum head of blonde hair, darker at the roots, was teased and dry, and she moved her face left-right under it like a theatrical queen under her crown, while clenching her lower jaw, as if holding back something dangerous in her neck that mustn't get out, and aiming her upward-looking eyes constantly at the heads of her guests. Her very thin eyebrows arched in a sort of deliberately arranged surprise when she jutted her chin at me and asked, "So what's up, Hrabrovka?" "Not much," I said, unsuccessfully fixing my gaze on a small piece of meat I was mangling with my dull knife, "just came home for a bit." She eyed me solemnly for several minutes. I knew she'd already noticed how often I was looking at the little street between her house and the church that led to our house. She glanced at the red marks on my hands. "We'll take care of everything," she said softly, wetly smacking her lips. She pointed her chin at the two boys sitting next to me, then wagged her head and smiled reprovingly with a little something that could be called tenderness. "Ivo Jureško, bite down harder," she sternly addressed the shorter of the two, who was listlessly pushing the lamb around in his mouth. He, a boy in early puberty, had Zvjezdana's coarse facial features and broad shoulders, while the taller one, a boy of sixteen or seventeen, took after his father physically. Apparently neither of them had inherited her particular character. On they chewed, engrossed, battling with each mouthful. "Jureško's blood," she said, "always needs a little push." "Beanpole here," she pointed her chin at the taller boy, "one day he came home, nose to the ground. His girlfriend had taken up with another boy. A flibbertigibbet, the Grzun girl. Fine, I say to him, so be it when you're such a whining little cunt, but I want you to put on this table right here everything you ever bought for her. That he couldn't do. Well, fuck it all, I said, now you'll see how it's done. I dragged him over to the Grzuns, knocked on the door, and explained nice as can be to the people that my boy was a useless fool." She stopped to swallow a bite, watching her son, who, one could feel without even looking at him, had wrapped himself around his plate. "You think I didn't get all of it back?" She ran down the list with a sneer of disgust. "The chains with the little hearts, and the gold earrings, and the purse, and the silk blouses, the dolphin, the stuffed teddy bears." Then she stopped, and the weight of all the things she'd listed dropped onto the table, and I felt even more so that the food I was eating was hers. "I never fight, I'm a very fine lady," she added. "These two, the Kojićes," she jutted her chin toward her father and brother, "now that's a different story altogether." Then she started randomly describing various problems they brought her every day and the solutions to the same which followed very quickly. She talked about them as if they weren't there. Her brother—a wan, dazed forty-year-old in a faded T-shirt, who, for the last two decades, had looked as if he'd just been dragged up from the cellar where he'd been playing video games for years and was confused and angry at the glare and people's voices—was sitting very close to his father, listening to the mumbled requests, handing him bread, a napkin, meat, a toothpick, pouring him wine and water, nodding at his comments. Both of them looked as if they had no idea that Zvjezdana was talking about them. Only her father glanced over at me with those eyes of his, to which old age had brought nothing good. His calculation had turned into fear, and he said, "What's your daddy up to, Ms. Ćosić?" "She's Gorana Hrabrov, Old Man. Her daddy died," Zvijezda yelled in his ear. "When?" gawked the old man. She looked at him and nodded her head in his direction, as if to say, see what I have to deal with? "Nobody ever listens to me, Hrabrovka, my friend," she said in her martyr's voice, with such affect that it wasn't clear whether she was being ironic or not. Now she was holding a bone and nibbling the meat off it, and her fat fingers, cluttered with gold rings and bright-red nail polish, looked a little silly while from them she was trying to extract, in the way she touched the napkins or raised the glasses, a sort of elegance. Chewing with dedication, she told me about her job at the ferry port, where she was in charge of the largest store on the island. Did I know how delicate this job is? You need to be a psychologist and a sociologist and a special brand of artist. "We get this delivery of underwear, men's, and it's red, no less. I tell them straightaway: take it back, nobody here will wear it. The big bosses say put them out on the shelves. I put them out—nothing sold," she said and shot me a knowing glance over the bone. "While in other places," she swung her arm above her head as if indicating all the other islands, "they sold out on day one." She leaned over and whispered confidentially, "Faggots, every last one of them." She set down the gnawed bone, sat back, and started watching the guests at the table. She caught their eyes, nodded and smiled, and then shook her head, as if sharing with each one an appealing and slightly embarrassing secret. Sometimes she'd declare something to someone, a sentence like "Live it up, way to go!" or "Salty enough for you?" but she said these with such a cozy, cunning smile that each word, even the most ordinary, was laden with meaning and conferred on each guest a special air of importance, which held true only as far as Zvijezda meant it to. If a person were to trust his privileged position and grow bolder, tossing across the table sentiments he considered witty or interesting, she'd retreat, half shut her eyes as if dozing, and dig, with a toothpick, at the crooked teeth poking out ominously from between her lips—frozen in a grimace resembling incensed disgust—and then the teeth would vanish when she compressed her lips in a line, apathetic, sad at the corners; from there two creases would move up toward her nose, and each superfluous word would splash down onto the table like unpleasant rain that was out to spoil everything, and he who'd spoken would shut up and squeeze himself into the size befitting him. Zvijezda would then glance up, and with quiet satisfaction she'd peruse her kingdom in which every subject was ruled by the law she'd laid down.

"Have you seen my man?" she asked me at one moment, pointing to her husband, who, tall and stooped, was sitting at the other end of the table next to an elderly man and woman, probably his parents, who were perched there stiffly as if they'd come from another country and not from somewhere nearby. He ate without looking up from his plate. "Not the sharpest one, as well you know," she said, "but he's like a mule—strong and hardworking."

Her gaze circled around the table as if she were thinking long and hard, and then she went on to say, in confidence, "Why not finish the roof while you're here? You can work on those drafts you do, and Jureško will build whatever you like. Pay when you can." She drew back slowly, and quietly watched me with a note of challenge. "I'm serious," she added. There are people like her, Hladna, who are appalling in the way they bind together their steel words and succeed, with no resistance, in ensnaring the person they're speaking with, but they are able to bend even the most unpleasant part of reality to their will, until the person suddenly feels their unenviable position as a point from which they can move in any direction and achieve success. Why, indeed, not do the roof? The rational part of me knew this was impossible, and yet I couldn't come up with a good reason for turning down Zvijezda's offer. "We'll see," I mumbled. Several times, she shot a glance at my sensitive fingers, so quickly and mercilessly that I flinched and dropped my hands onto my lap. She sighed slowly, as if she didn't know what to do with me, but right afterward she leaned over on her elbow and said, almost gently, "But what am I telling you..." as if I'd already agreed. I took out a new chunk of meat just to keep busy with something and occupied myself with cutting it; meanwhile, Zvijezda went off to the house to bring out more wine for the younger guests, probably her nephews, who had been waving to her for some time from the other end of the table. When she came back, she personally served them the wine and stayed with them, all coy and playful, and I began thinking about leaving the festivities. I had a look at how afternoon shadow was beginning to take over the narrow street between the church and Zvijezda's house. A little more. A little more patience, and the afternoon would soften the space, soften the edges of our house and make the yard dark enough for me to trust it and well enough lit for me to preserve the vague hope I was feeling. I looked at the guests. Their shiny metal voices held the shadow of the umbrella high over the table, but the stains from grease and olive oil mixed with vinegar and upsetting traces of tomatoes had already interrupted the superior whiteness of the tablecloth in places. Smeared lipstick, blackened flesh under fingernails, chests bared. Soon Zvjezdana's sister's unwieldy gold necklace would acquire its afternoon patina, and jaws would chew the cake more slowly. "I never liked your daddy much, Ms. Ćosić," old Kojić said defiantly and raised his arms as if expecting me to hit him. I nodded and smiled. His son whispered something to him, which quieted him down, but he went on watching me from under his wild eyebrows, distrustful and dark. Zvijezda came back to her seat. She was breathing shallowly, retreating from the affection she clearly felt for her nephews to more amenable behavior. She seemed to be pondering something. I didn't catch the moment when she shot a glance across the table at her husband, but she must have, because Jureško suddenly showed up between us. She crooked a finger as a signal for him to come closer and crooked the same finger to me. "Hrabrovka here has come to fix the roof," she said. "Go over to Nakić's tomorrow, why don't you, and pick up everything you'll need." "But no, no," I stammered with an awkward smile. "What? You'd rather buy the construction materials yourself?" Zvijezda broke in with disgruntled surprise, almost sharply. Jureško looked at me with a dose of caution, as if he were a little afraid of what

I might decide. His goggly gray eyes dominated his narrow face and oddly undermined the firm resolve implied by his low, graying hairline, and there was something carefree that settled along the rims of his big ears. It was impossible for him to hide those eyes of his; no matter where he looked, Zvijezda would find them and stab him mercilessly with her sly gaze. In front of others, he was salvaged by the pout of his lower lip. It gave him, with his tall and mildly hunched posture, a slightly off-putting look, the defense mechanism of a teenager who, though insecure, a bit gullible, and essentially well-meaning, couldn't help but feel a little spiteful disdain for all who weren't part of his clique. "We'll see what condition the house is in," I heard myself say. "Let's not go buying anything just yet." Jureško and Zvijezda exchanged looks. "Well, okay," she said with feigned disappointment, the way she'd concede to the person she was talking with, while also hinting that everything would turn out exactly like she said. Jureško waited briefly, unsure, and then went back to his seat, and Zvijezda poured wine for herself and me. She was quiet. "So, how's Kiddo?" she asked, without looking my way. Where did the cold tenderness of that question come from? From childhood, when she was still pretending she wasn't in love with Kiddo, but it probably took its final form in the second half of the 1990s, after their brief relationship ended, and she finally had to admit defeat. I watched her while she stared at the dark-red surface of the wine. Our Zvijezda tried everything; while still underage, she enlisted in the army in 1991, then earned a diploma from the teachers college through her party ties, but she couldn't grasp that my brother wouldn't be wowed by the courage or brains of someone else. "Just look at how our priest has his eye on you," she whispered. Her pupils floated in the bloodshot ooze over the whites of her eyes. "Don Jebo!" she called across the table. "Anything catch your eye?" This flustered the young priest; he sipped some wine and laughed nervously. Now he was being too lively, like a puppet which, with the bright red of its cheeks and the assertive shine of its eyes, from its powerful urge to appear healthy, comes across, instead, as sick. He had, indeed, been looking at me; he couldn't hide this even after he'd been outed. I looked over at Zvijezda and laughed. "I found you a fuckmate," she said. Two girls, the ones who had served the lamb, now cleared the dirty plates and took them back to the house. Zvijezda watched them, planted on her elbows, until finally she also got up and cleared the platters with what was left of the meat. At first the wine she'd been drinking left her looking tired, but when she brought out the cake and coffee, she perked up. "At the corner stands a house, a modest house, my friends," she sang, belting out the popular song so suddenly that it gave me goose bumps. The table joined in. "And in it Ana counts the days, counts the nights, my friends" reverberated on all sides. The chorus was awful, but, still, I didn't leave. The afternoon marked the day with its festive identity, and undertaking anything seemed unreasonable. Zvijezda put her left hand on the shoulder of the young priest, who couldn't stop blushing, while she conducted the song with her right. She no longer paid me any attention, but her sister watched me in secret. Stiff, silent, in black, she looked like the embodiment of Zvjezdana's invisible side, and with her cautious presence she made all the lighthearted, rousing folk songs sound plodding.

The lace on Irma's panties was chafing me. I ate a piece of chocolate cake with cherries that filled my stomach in such a way that my body began to feel as if it were done. I tried to have some coffee but couldn't. The time really had come for me to go home. I got up, waved briefly to everyone without looking at anyone, and headed toward the little street I'd been eyeing the whole while from the table, stepping quickly enough that Zvijezda didn't have the chance to stop the song and come up with more problems she'd have to solve for me. I didn't have far to go. Our house stood at the end of the little street I'd stepped into, only some thirty meters from the square. The familiar facade with four windows on the two floors, so run-down that you could no longer be sure what the original color had been; up above, flapping in the wind, the black plastic sheeting that had been nailed down to cover the open roof; a tall, two-part courtyard door, always painted in a reddish-brown, rust-like hue. I peeked through the largest hole in the door panel, but the front part of the yard was in shadow, and there was mottled light farther off on the summer terrace. The time had come to go in, I thought, and took a deep breath. The iron hinges creaked when I turned the handle. Though anticipated, tears welled up inside me at the endearing unpleasantness of the sound. Underfoot I felt the envelopes of bills the postman had pushed under the door, but I didn't lean over to collect them. I advanced slowly and cautiously. The narrow part of the yard—with the older house on the right and the more recent one-story wing on the left—was, as always, piled high with stuff in the corners and along the walls, whether handy things like a broom and shovel, fishing nets, and a container with seeds, or useful trash, such as old shoes for working in the garden and worn-out kitchen towels, and then the odds and ends that only houses with a deep history know: the useless objects that have earned their place simply by having been here for too long, like the cardboard model of a happy chef that Father brought from a restaurant he'd sold fish to. The passage was protected by an overhang, reaching from the old house all the way to the smaller eaves of the newer wing, so all these things were surprisingly well-preserved and dry. The thick carpet of fallen leaves began only in the second part of the yard, which was wider and more open, and was covered only by rows of terraced grapevines, now quite an autumnal yellow, which had here and there strayed from their guide wires. The lopsided shed still stood behind the house to the right. Behind it the garden had gone to weed; only a few rogue tomato plants had survived, along with brittle cabbage stalks. To the left—a large, wooden, rectangular table surrounded by chairs of the most varied shapes and sizes, materials, and colors, stained with residue from dried figs and bird shit. A sooty hearth. Next to it, in the corner, a fig tree that had bested the grapevine in several incursions and was now glowing confidently about being able to take over as much of the yard as it wanted within the year. I brushed the leaves off the nearest chair and sat down, watching the tender play of the light. Everything around me was familiar in both a comfortable and an uncomfortable way, like meeting someone I used to be close to a long time ago. I felt a quiet joy in my eyes, but if the walls, grapevine, or shed was expecting me to say something, I couldn't. I was by myself there for the first time. Yes. No matter how far I went back in my memories, even to the earliest times,

I couldn't recall a single day, even hour, when I had been by myself in this house: I pictured sunburned Mate and Kiddo with his first whiskers, smoking and drinking at this very table; Milka making the rounds of the geraniums with a charming yellow watering can; Zoran sitting by the door to his room, piling up seashells in plastic boxes; Irma calling; Ante and Jere on their way back from town; Rina and Martina arriving from Ljubljana; sisters and brothers-in-law coming; new nephews being born—and all I could do was retreat to my room in the newer wing. Its door opened directly onto the yard. Only a thin partition separated my room from the bathroom, and there was always somebody on their way in or out. It was strange, now, to see this place free of family for the first time, to examine its true dimensions and features. I studied the dead flies floating around a candle for repelling mosquitoes, which sat in a water-filled ceramic dish in the middle of the table. The afternoon was on the wane. When I decided to pick up the dish with both hands and dump the water, candle, and floating flies under the grapevine—was this the moment when I realized I was still an architect? This was a baseline architectural feeling, much like the compulsion of a caveman to take a rock and destroy the spike poking him in the head at his cave entrance. But, Hladna, what is an architect after all? An ape who cannot tolerate being held back by falling leaves. I have no better definition. Right, I thought, first, tidy everything up, return to human purpose, show the fig tree who's the boss here. I grabbed the broom and swept the leaves from the table, chairs, and ground into a pile by the edge of the garden. I climbed up onto the table and tucked the stray grapevine back onto its guide wires. I gathered up the bills. My drafts of the house, I thought, I must find the drafts I'd made two years before. I knew that the room where I'd left them, "my room," wasn't locked, but I couldn't bring myself to go and get them. It's not that I was scared about facing my childhood. There had never been enough of me in that space for me to feel that kind of fear. Built in the second half of the 1970s, and along with the bathroom and a room for Kiddo in his rightful place, up on the second floor, next to Granny Palma, this had always been a place designed for people passing through. A bed for Maria so she could come back after secondary school to work at the fish-processing plant, a bed for Anica before she moved into town, a bed for Irma and Zoran until they found a home of their own, a bed for the nephews who were hiding out from the war or spending their summer vacation here, a bed for me, the unplanned-for latecomer. What I was scared of now was being faced with its cold rationality. And indeed, when I went in, I encountered the bloodless feel of the place, partway between a monastery and a homeless shelter. The white walls, the musty smell, the cheap bunk beds with plaid bedspreads. The narrow view of the yard through the little window, so much like a bathroom window. Several forgotten books, random trifles pinned to the corkboard that had been crammed in above the desk, a pink plush toy—a piglet—on the pillow that matched nothing else in the room. A wardrobe of uncertain origins. I took the drafts from the desk and sat on the lower bunk to have a look. On the blanket, I arranged the sheets of paper side by side. These were sketches I'd made by hand, messy and puzzling to decipher in spots, and it took me a while to realize that these were in fact at least ten to fifteen different versions of the imagined house, and I couldn't tell which I'd thought was best. How is it possible, I wondered, that I, who had always worked with care, had left such disorder behind? I stared at the familiar handwriting, my handwriting, which didn't feel like mine at all. The day was growing darker, but I knew there was no point in trying to turn on a light—the electricity had certainly long since been shut off. If only Igor were here, I thought, we read each other's drafts with an unflinching eye. He'd know what I'd meant to say. I could picture him there before me as he was when he was a student: skinny and slightly hunched, his long, thick eyelashes giving his face something of a girlish sweetness. In his mind a rumpled boy, in his body a grown architect; his clothing was somewhere halfway between the two. Dwelling easily in the soft curls of his hair and beard, yet capable of mercilessly slicing any setting he disliked with his green eyes. There had been a silent recognition between us from the start. We only rarely conversed, but in the lecture hall, in the cafeteria, or at the social gatherings we seldom shared, we were always aware of each other's presence. How do I know this? By his voice, Hladna. His voice was unique, like an instrument that cannot decide what it is, the voice of a buddy going arm in arm with his restless gaze, always gauging the place and people, a voice in flux, ending most often in an unsettling polyphony. But when he felt me listening, his voice would change to become like a big drum which, calm and sure in its dark interiority, allowed the natural flow of air to vibrate its membrane ever so slightly, while offering me its light, outward-facing side, as if challenging me by giving me a delicate spot where I could tap in response, but only if I wanted to. For a few years after we graduated, we weren't in touch at all, but I can't say I was truly surprised when he came looking for me when I was working for the Old Man after my emerging architect award and suggested that I could go work for Elena Sajko. This was in 2011, and he had already brought a certain freshness to Elena's otherwise stagnant architectural bureau on Črnomerec. We struggled to push a third desk into the tiny room next to her apartment, piled high with drafts and too cramped for two, let alone three. Elena was already over sixty and weary of her lifelong travail, having always been the odd person out as a woman, a democrat, a leftist, having to justify her existence over and over again. "Sooner or later, we'll crack these nutmegs wide open, won't we?" she'd say and wink at me while playfully squeezing Igor's head in the pincers of her short, plump fingers. From the beginning, because of her bad knee and achy spine, or because of the depression that followed the aches and pains, she didn't often come to work. She'd call us from her apartment to bring her the medicine and ice cream she needed, or to take Gropius, her Great Dane, out for a walk in the park by her building. But her presence, though frail, dark, and shadowy in a room smelling of old newspapers, had the effect of giving Igor and me the feeling that we were really young. Zagreb had begun with us. We had the good fortune in the first few years of winning several bids for desirable projects. These were generally public spaces of lesser importance, not particularly attractive for the better-known studios, and they allowed us to show, without pretension, what we could do. A small outdoor food market in New Zagreb, an Upper Town nursery school, several expansions of older buildings, a park on Pešćenica. Igor had a better feel for people; he was able to find the points where the chaotic lines of human emotions intersected, while I had a better feel for the space and worked to preserve its integrity, both in terms of structural constraints and the demands of design intent. In 2015, we received the Viktor Kovačić Award for a new wing we designed for an elementary school in Kozari Putevi. Now, as I lay on my childhood bed, I tried to summon the special atmosphere of the evening when we celebrated that success. After the ceremony and reception, I drove them both home. Elena got out in front of her building on Črnomerec and invited us up for another drink, but both of us quickly declined. It was clear that she was exhausted from too much joy, and slightly tipsy. We watched her lurch between the rectangular shrubs around the entranceway. She reminded me of a hedgehog returning to its dark lair after making its nocturnal rounds, and this revived for me scenes from childhood when I'd pull one such vulnerable animal from an island hole and let it proceed along its way. Igor and I sat next to each other, the streetlamps gave the quiet road and trees a velvety look, and I knew he was feeling the same quiet tenderness as he watched Elena disappear into her building's darkness. We'd been managing, without knowing how, to save this creature anew every day, offering her yet another chance to flaunt for the public her impressive hedgehog spines, and then to creep back safely to the shelter she needed. I turned off the car. "Igor, do you think we did everything we could with the floor in that school?" He was quiet for a bit before saying, "What do you mean?" Oh, he'd understood me; his voice told me so. "I am thinking of the conundrum of flooring for schools," I said. "Choosing the right material is impossible. Tiles are too cold, laminate is too weak and noisy, wood costs too much. The only logical choice is linoleum. It's cheap and easy to maintain. But linoleum is so awful. It's the material of bureaucracy. The gray compromise." "There's no way to be an uncompromising architect," he said, a little protectively. I looked at him. "I thought that's what we've been working for," I said. He sighed. "But what would you use instead of linoleum?" "Well, I don't know," I said, "what about dirt, a la the Japanese?" He laughed aloud. "Why not?" I wheedled. "Let the kids prance around. Or maybe pebbles. Or rocks. Let them hop around like baby goats." We laughed and then got serious. "The only compromise we need to work on is ours with nature," I said softly, looking out at the empty street. "You must have learned that from Wright. Our task is to tame the space enough to assuage human fear. The discomfort of physical existence." "We must cooperate with utility as well, and with the human subconscious," he said dryly. "But not with deliberate lies," I added. I didn't realize I'd been tilting to the right until I felt his warmth. He was sitting very close to me. We looked at each other. How can I ever forget the cold magnificence of that moment? No, he didn't look at me the way he did many years later at the symposium, as something outside of himself. Will I be clear enough, Hladna, if I say he didn't actually see me with his eyes but with his very presence? It was as if his body were watching me, the dark, invisible part of him, his organs that didn't know my name but knew the anxious rhythm of my breathing, the angry pulse of blood to the brain, the way I digested what I ingested. I placed my palm over his hand. The back of his hand was dry, protected by hair, but when he turned it and allowed me to slip my fingers into the spaces between his fingers, I was met by the warm moisture of his skin and I sensed the car more strongly where we were sitting, the coarse presence of the fabric underneath us, the plastic-steel-glass structure of the old Peugeot surrounding us. Igor's body in that immobile, inorganic environment seemed so frangible, with sweaty palms and a pulse shakily marching onward to its end. I felt the inadequacy of his skin, its terrible powerlessness to protect us. Igor tenderly cupped the back of my neck with his palm and brought my face so close, I could feel his breath, but too late. I withdrew my right hand from his, laid my left on his chest and gently pushed him away. Then, after all, I unbuttoned the first two buttons on his shirt. Then buttoned up the second one. We pulled back from each other. "I'll take you to Trešnjevka," I said, staring at the steering wheel, as if he didn't already know I would. "Fine," he said, in a voice that sounded as if it were coming from the bleakest part of me. After that evening, everything changed. Soon we moved into a larger office on Gundulićeva Street and were given more important commissions. A whole school in Zagorje, a new hotel in the center of town. Elena rarely joined us, two or three times a month, if that, and we stopped by her apartment less often. Formally, Igor was the boss, but we made all our decisions together, feeling the difficulties of the process more and more. It was, of course, impossible for us not to work for wealthy private clients, but I felt we must protect our authorship from bad compromises, because we owed much to the built environment, while Igor was more inclined to respect the wishes of those who were footing the bill. We no longer referred to our jobs as "house," "school," or "hotel," but "project." In the big new office, we sat meters apart, and soon we began filling the space with people: a male trainee, a female trainee, a secretary. From the greater distance, observing Igor was easy, and I could see there was so much in him that I didn't recognize as mine: his easygoing father, a psychiatrist, and his strict mother, a music teacher; his early childhood in New Zagreb, on the vast meadow that still believed it could become anything; then his parents' divorce, growing up in the center of town in an apartment with high ceilings that forced you to aspire to something more elevated; his dark-haired mother with her cats and Macedonian accent—sometimes too present, sometimes too absent; his father's new marriages, his half brothers and half sisters; his girlfriends—nothing serious, a medical student with whom he lived for three years; his bachelor existence on Trešnjevka; and, finally, Slavica, whom he met soon after we moved our office to Gundulićeva. Did all this have to lead to the midlife fear that he might lose the comfortable existence he'd known? With quiet horror I watched how his student passion for the radical mastery of space—spurred by his unerring sense for the affective potential of every wall, window, or tile—became an empty gesture, an exploitation of his skill. He became the most ordinary draftsman of blueprints. Am I becoming that, I wondered. No, I insisted, I'm still capable of sabotaging the homes of the wealthy from within, to build the megalomaniacal mindset of their owners into solutions which, though aesthetically correct at first glance, make the space maliciously vengeful and undermine the long term inhabitant: hallways that greet coldly; the too-long distance from toilet to bathtub, leaving a person time to dwell on the superiority of their own physiology; rooms with an imposed character that always seems alien. And besides, I thought, I'm designing single-family homes, small houses for small people, attending honestly to the balance of space and human nature. But whenever I looked in the mirror, I knew why I regularly straightened my hair and added highlights, used moderate but normal makeup, wore spotlessly clean suit jackets and expensive shoes, went for manicures and depilation: to make my external form opaque, even to my own gaze. Do you remember, Hladna, when I wrote there at the restaurant, at dinner with Marta and her husband, that the thought of Igor's shaved cheeks filled me with a dread I couldn't put my finger on? Now, in the darkness of my childhood bedroom, I knew where that feeling had come from. I could vividly summon the day, three years before, and the moment when he came into the office with radically shorter hair, clean-shaven. "How do I look?" he asked. "For the first time, I see you have a flat nose," I said. His nose truly did seem flatter, but that wasn't what had disturbed me. It was the way his immobile porcelain jaw sat upon his short neck with the bearing of a proper gentleman. When his hair had been tousled, it functioned as an unusual but welcome counterweight to his body, with its otherwise conventional proportions and modest limitations of movement, but now the body had merged with the head as a singular whole, permanently defined and utterly predictable. We were alone that day at the office, working late. We had to come up with a solution for a wing on the Vargek house, a building that was unfixable, with a tower of some sort and a facade of marble cladding. "Igor," I said, "should we give up on this one?" "Why?" he asked. His voice no longer held the tenor of the transparent drum. More often, as it did that day, it defied comparison with any musical instrument. Where had that self-satisfied half smile, which never left his face anymore, suddenly come from? "Because," I said, trying to sound calm, "this house doesn't look like a house, but like a luxury shithole. Hopeless." "We don't always get a blank sheet of paper," he said, "but we need to make the most with what we have." "Fuck this!" I spat and threw my pen onto the desk. We stopped talking and avoided looking at each other. I waited for my breathing to slow. "We are becoming an invasive species," I said. "Apprentices who help the wealthy occupy space. We're making Zagreb, this country, the world, permanently ugly. Or what's worse: we're lying for them, developing a false modernism that is designed to portray them as better than they are." "If you thought you'd be waging a revolution, you shouldn't have chosen architecture. You know full well it doesn't have the capacity for critique," he said, without any sort of smile. I fell silent, thinking of how best to formulate what I wanted to say. "I'm not talking about that. I'm not talking about that at all. I am talking about how we used to make fun of the architects we're now becoming. How we tried, as much as possible, to come up with spatial solutions offering a shelter of sorts in the face of the implacable laws of transience. Havens allowing each person to feel the city as their own. Public spaces that might give some self-awareness. We tried to create tenderness amid the cruelty, strength amid the weakness. And now... now we're like Frank Lloyd Wright in his crisis phase." I knew I'd stung him in the right place when his face winced at the mention of Wright's beloved name. Oh, yes, I wanted to destroy Saint Wright, that ninety-year-old man standing atop the Guggenheim Museum. To place on his shoulders Ennis House and Hollyhock House and let him carry them if he wasn't ashamed of their Sezession concrete blocks. I wanted to burn down his Taliesin I and Taliesin II and Taliesin III, kill Mamah Borthwick and her children again, disassemble Frank Lloyd into his composite parts, to force Igor to look into the darkness hiding there within him. "All of Wright's houses should be considered from the other side," I said, "like structures sustaining an oligarchic vision of society." He didn't look at me. "We know what brought about Le Corbusier's exaggerated concern for the collective," he said. He was furious; this was obvious from the red flush spreading across his forehead. His eyes were tearing up, his lips pursing, his nose growing more pointed, but he remained implacable. No matter how hard I tried, I could no longer find my way to that voice of his, which had been like a transparent drum. I really couldn't touch him. I got up, took my coat and bag. "Le Corbusier at least tried to include all people," I said softly. Then I left the office. If only this had been my final exit, if I hadn't come back the next day, at least. Nothing of what I'm telling you would have happened. I'd have been forced to open my own firm and start a new life. But I wasn't ready yet for severing ties, out of fear, curiosity, or masochism, who knows. I thought about it while lying there on top of my drafts in the dark room, and at one moment, sleep tricked me. I woke up when it was still night. Why, of course, I thought, now I know why I couldn't come up with the right solution for how to renovate our house. Not because it would have been impossible to recast the architectural amateurism of my predecessors in an aesthetically acceptable way, but because there is no spatial balance that would satisfy every member of my family. This building—of bits and pieces patched together out of necessity, with whatever materials were available just then, now parts of it crumbling, parts of it unfinished, a little cold, a little warm—was perhaps the most precise articulation of our relationships. Hadn't I realized back then, two years before, that my creativity was entirely powerless when faced with the chaotic nature of the building? Perhaps the only proper solution, I thought, was to conserve it as it was, and turn the house into a monument of sorts to who I was. Who we were. I began, at first just for fun, to play with thoughts about Zvjezdana's proposal to finish the roof. I remembered the beams I'd noticed buried in leaves, under the grapevines and roof tiles, deep in the weeds taking over a corner of the garden, and I realized I already had most of the materials I'd need. I remembered that in Milka and Mate's bedroom, there might be some gold stashed away or Milka's hidden cash for emergencies. I remembered that the key that opened the old house was in the toilet tank mounted on the bathroom wall, and, like the rest of the new building, the bathroom was never locked. I don't know when I decided to go and fetch the key, but I do know that I found myself at one moment standing tiptoe in the dark on the toilet seat, groping around in the slimy insides of the tank. The stench of stagnant water and mildew was so strong, I felt it eating at my fingers. When I touched the plastic baggie and pulled out the key, something like a shiver of excitement shot through me. Moving warily in the dark, I came to the front door of the old house and worked the key into the lock. It caught slightly, the wood grumbled in a way I knew, but the door did let me in. I stepped into the hallway. There was a recognizable fragrance, the fragrance of our house, but mixed with the smell of the damp, it seemed colder and gave the impression of an expansive indifference. I saw nothing but darkness, yet I knew all the things were where they should be. Shoes in the hall, the kitchen behind the door straight ahead, the living room with the couch, the table, the stove, and the television behind the door on the left kitchen wall. Mate's Stjepan Radić over the TV set, Milka's poppies in a gold frame over the couch. The wooden stairs to my left. Up I went to the second floor. Although the carpeting tamped my steps in its familiar thin way, I felt as if I were disturbing the house, and the bedrooms knew I was coming. Behind the door to the left, Milka and Mate were waiting for me in their wedding portrait over the head of the bed. I felt their young eyes following me through the dark while I rummaged through the bedding in the cupboards, trying to find the gold or the money. I patted everything. Nothing there—only socks and old prayer books in the drawers. I sat on the bed, thinking. The plastic sheeting above the thin woven-reed ceiling drummed away in the night breeze, as if the house were rebelling. I looked under the bed. Nothing. Only when I was on my way out, and the threshold creaked under my weight, did I remember. In one spot, with a little skill, some pieces of the parquet flooring under the bed could be pried up. I did this and uncovered the hole, and there, after scooping aside the rubble, I felt a leather bag and a flat box. Then I went downstairs with them, groped around for matches in the kitchen, went out into the yard, and lit a candle on the table. The bag and the box were there in front of me. Had I already known I wouldn't use what I found there to keep on running away? I had, Hladna. You're probably asking why. I can't explain it other than to ask you: Have you ever done something which seems at first glance to fly in the face of all logic, yet you knew it was exactly correct and the only thing possible? Yes, and I also knew I had to clean up and put to rights the house of my childhood. This was the only proper thing to do just then. I took a deep breath and opened the bag and the box. In the bag, as expected, there were many containers holding family gold, while in the box I found kunas, euros, and dollars totaling over 62,000 kunas. I came up with a plan for the renovation. I'd finish the roof, paint the house inside and out, restore the furniture, work on the garden and the shed. By daybreak, I took some of the money, stowed the rest away in the kitchen, and locked the house. I took the bus to the ferry port, and at the post office I paid the rent for my Zagreb apartment, and then, without delay, I returned to the village. Zvijezda's table was still out on the square, covered with the dirty tablecloth, whipped around by the sea wind, with several empty bottles left here and there and the floral bouquets in the middle. I saw her through the open door, bent over her kitchen sink. I went over and knocked on the doorframe. She turned. "Hrabrovka, where did you run off to yesterday?" she said groggily. "When can Jureško begin?" "And where's your computer?" She was startled but made an effort not to show it. Fixing her eyes on her dishes, she said breezily, "Jureško can start right away. The laptop is in the living room, and it's on." I sat at the screen, collected my thoughts for a few minutes, and then wrote an email to my landlord. I'd paid the rent; I hoped he didn't mind that I hadn't been in touch; I'd left all of my devices in the apartment when I had to leave town suddenly because of a serious family situation. As soon as I could catch a moment and find a phone, I'd call. If anything urgent came up, he should use email to reach me. You see, Hladna, it's not that I was pulling a fast one; I had decided in all seriousness to trust the story of my own innocence. The island, I'm telling you, the island had my back. It declared the only thing that exists is what is here around you right now: Zvijezda's dark-red living room, her house, the square and street, the village, the sea. Nothing exists beyond this. If I had still been feeling anxiety the day before, by then it was gone. This is because loneliness doesn't stay sitting on your chest on an island. It collaborates with the space around you to lighten things up. It wasn't that I could no longer imagine the police coming for me, but now I felt my guilt was outside of me. If they come, I decided, I'll accept the consequences, as if embracing an unpleasant obligation. I'll admit it to you now: they didn't come for me that whole autumn and winter. How to describe those nearly six island months? The days were one much like another, but there was in each one a lovely, slightly childish, freshness. I slept in the new wing of the house, in the other bedroom, Zoran and Irma's, where there was more light. The autumn was warm, with abundant sunlight, and until the winter began, I could still eat my breakfast outside, under the grapevine, its leaves turning yellow and red, provocatively lavish in its beauty, knowing it was condemned to the forthcoming rains. In the morning, the day was still uncertain, and they easily could have come to take me in. I waited for them calmly and coldly, only a little flustered, focusing on the weeds, cleaning the bathroom, picking through the trash, chores that ushered a sense of order into the chaotic scramble of thought. After lunch, at two or three in the afternoon, Jureško would come over, alone or with one or both of his boys, and we'd start working on the roof. Sometimes, if the forecast called for rain, he'd bring another worker who helped us anchor and reinforce the plastic sheeting. Zvijezda would stop by every few days, most often in the evenings, behaving as if we'd asked her to come so she could tell us what we'd been doing wrong. Every few weeks she'd bring along a bottle of homemade wine, and she'd sit with a glass and deliver long monologues about the chronic incompetence of Jureško and all Kojićes. "How's Kiddo?" she'd always ask at the end. This bothered me, the same way people are bothered by pesky flies or aggressive wasps, but she couldn't upset me, because there was no longer a weak spot on me for her to poke at with her stinger. I was just a simple mason. Three or four times she brought news from Anica: Milka was continuing to live, unchanged. Sometimes Tome stopped by, always in a rush, and I had no trouble explaining why I'd stayed on the island, because he tended to believe everything. He was glad to arrange to have my electricity and water turned on and make sure I had enough wood to heat the house. Two or three times the young priest stopped by, blushing and muttering about the importance of attending Sunday Mass. I found it amusing to flirt with him, to see how naively he took the bait, and then I'd abruptly pull back and act so insulted, I put fear in his bones, and then he'd give lengthy explanations about this not being what he'd meant. This was probably quite childish of me, but a person has to have a hobby. Winters on the island are long, as you probably know. We only finished the roof right before Christmas and began working on the facade. Now that the days were shorter, Jureško wasn't as able to make time after his regular workday, so I did much of the work myself. Besides, he was so untalkative during the time I did spend with him, I felt as if I were working alone. At dusk, I'd go down to the waterfront, sit on one of the benches, and watch the sea and the city, which lit up across the water. There was a kind of good intimacy in the way the fishermen worked around their boats or the occasional young mothers pushed their strollers, calmly and easily, despite my presence, about which they knew little. But what I enjoyed the most were those moments when a flock of gulls would fly up over the other shore, and when, lit by the city lights, the birds against the blue background looked like sparks. "The past is always blue," wrote Charles-Édouard Jeanneret in a letter, "the present is red and yellow, like fire, a house in flames." Le Corbusier, you white raven, I thought, you who dared shape our lives, to light a fire and escape to your cabin on the shore, how did you manage to disappear into the sea, yet not die? I'd sit that way for a half hour or hour and then go home, prepare something to eat, and work on drawings until I went to bed, trying to create what I called "the house I'll build if I ever build houses again" or "the ideal building." You're probably wondering how I managed to survive all those months on the money I found. Frugally, I have to say. I ate local fish and vegetables, accepted all the food Zvijezda or Tome brought me, as was the good village custom, wore my old sweats that I found in a cupboard and Milka's roomy white underpants, was parsimonious with electricity and water, and was rational with the building costs. Beyond the cost of materials, my largest outlay every month was rent for the apartment on Medveščak, but I went on stubbornly paying it because my landlord hadn't been in touch. I felt as if, with each rent payment, I was buying time. Sometimes I wondered why he hadn't turned me in, why they hadn't come for me yet when he clearly knew where I was, but, honestly, I had far too much work to do to dwell on this. I was a simple mason—muscular, modest, with tough fingernails and calloused hands, where the red traces of the city bedbugs had long since disappeared. In February, when the first almond trees began to bloom on the island, I started with the interior renovation, quite independently. I painted the walls and parts of the furniture, cleared away the damage from two years of the damp. In March, when the official start of spring was near and the grapevines on the terrace had begun to bud, the renovation was done. Pleased, I walked from room to room. This is it, I thought. This is it. I couldn't remember the house ever looking like this, but it was, nevertheless, the same house. And much like the glorified version of my personal memories, it was agreeable, but I knew it wouldn't stay that way if I looked at it for too long. On the morning of the twenty-first, I returned the family gold to the hole under the parquet flooring, pulled on my white panties with the little black hearts, the dress I was wearing when I arrived, Anastazija's sneakers, and Milka's black coat, took my purse with the last 2,380 kunas, my documents, my sunglasses, and a bottle of water, locked up the old house and hid the key again in the water tank mounted on the bathroom wall, and then got into the car that Tome was driving to Zagreb with his wife to see her mother. You may be shocked by such an abrupt about-face. Why Zagreb, why now, you may wonder, as I said to Zvijezda and

Jureško, and why did I never end up going to see Zoran? I have no other way to answer than to say that a person must return, sooner or later, to the charred ruins and see what's left of their life. Zvijezda, Jureško, Zoran, they live on the island. I live in Zagreb, and I knew I had to return, though the familiar weight of loneliness was already percolating in my throat, and it was only a matter of time before it settled back down in my lungs. We left before eight, crossed on the ferry into town, and continued north on the highway. Lounging in the back seat, I watched Tome's tall, blonde wife—I didn't even know her name—fidget uncomfortably while listening to her husband talk about her mother, a Zagreb lady who apparently had been lamenting, ever since the quarantine began for the virus, about her miserable, lonely predicament, so they'd decided to drive up and bring her down to the island. Yes, of course, the topic of conversation was the new virus, "the one invented by the Chinese," the lockdown resulting from it, "and who knows what's next." I hardly knew anything about this, because I'd had no working television or internet on the island, so I kept quiet, only offering an occasional nod, engrossed in my own thoughts. In Dalmatia, the day was clear, but once we'd crossed over into Lika, the sky began clouding over. I watched the unhappy villages along the highway. "We are living in a country where the built environment has become so ugly, one cannot imagine a house that would be both good architecture and fitting well into the surroundings," I remembered from the beginning of my talk at the symposium. "This country, and perhaps every country in some way, is like that, and you have to decide whether you'll be a bad architect or a bad urbanist." Igor stood next to the audience in their seats and watched me, a little concerned, a little empathetic, a little anxious, a little mellow, but also with a dose of a good coldness, as if seeing me naked, without a trace of excitement. Our eyes met. I stopped. Now I know why he was looking at me that way, Hladna. Driving through Lika in the back seat of Tome's car, I summoned to memory our last client, a man whose house—honored with international awards—we were presenting at the symposium. Kutleša, maybe you've heard of him. Yes, that Kutleša, the have-fun-shopping Kutleša. Even now, at this distance, I couldn't find in his manner anything genuinely disturbing. Reasonably attractive, a trim haircut, graying around the edges, good taste in clothing and shoes, moderate in speech and gestures, he was more like one of those polished new age managers who stroll into glass office buildings every day than like the kings of this and that industry who paraded through our office. He was lacking the pushiness typical of those people, obvious even when they tried to hide it, and he looked more like a fancy version of a clerk than like an exploitative boss who got rich with shady wartime deals. What was it about him that troubled me so much? This may sound odd, but it was because I could find no fault with him. He didn't cling to failed architectural ideas, he accepted our suggestions with understanding, and our taste aligned well with his. The collaboration would have been quite a pleasant experience, if people like me could have trusted something other than their own restive spirit. Often, while we were working on the project, and afterward when it was recognized with awards, I thought of Wright's Fallingwater. What sort of man was Kaufmann, the businessman for whom the house was built, my uneasy spirit wanted to know.

And how much was Fallingwater ours, how much Wright's, and how much Kaufmann's? For, a house isn't a piece of art but a way of taming space, and ownership over it is not ownership of the view, but of fear. Only the chosen few can live in an architectural masterpiece, and the houses we patch together out of necessity, using whatever we have available, are what's left for the rest of us, these insecure houses, only partly finished and too cramped, always faster in decaying than we are. Perhaps Frank Lloyd, I thought, was more troubled on his deathbed by the masterpieces he'd built than the houses he'd built for money. I started harboring doubts, not only about what Igor and I were up to, but about the very essence of architecture. No, I said to myself, architecture for public use in general cannot save us; what we build is merely a feeble attempt to stave off the fear that erodes cities from within, in the houses, apartments, and rooms where people are born, then die, and then are born again. At the January symposium, before I went out onto the stage, I told Igor that I hadn't prepared what I'd promised to prepare about our project. Instead, I'd be giving a speech he might not like. We argued. He said I was taking things too far, that I always went too far, and, just like Elena, I was always acting the victim instead of accepting my gift and getting over my fear of success. "How can I not fear this success of yours," I said, "when it flies in the face of what I think success ought to be?" His green eyes stared coldly somewhere in the general direction of my left ear. "You're not the only one who matters. You are not the measure of all things," he said, choking back fury. Then he added, more calmly, "We need to do what we don't like so we can do what we like. That's how life works." Was I hearing a trace of the cherished transparent drum in his voice? Or was I just wanting to hear it? A moment later, while I was waiting to go onstage, standing next to Joško Dulčić, I squinted, to find out if by some miracle Igor's voice would show up right next to my ear and whisper to me that I was not alone. But the only things I sensed were the mothball odor from Dulčić's brown socialist suit and his wetly smacking words that had hardly anything to do with me. "Have you noticed, my young colleague," he said with a playful look, as if about to tell a bad joke, "that nature never makes a space ugly, only people do?" "That," I replied, more sharply than I meant to, "is because a tree is always a tree, while man generally thinks he's more consequential than he actually is." By the noise coming from his throat, I knew he was watching me with an open mouth. After a delay, he laughed. Then fell silent. He went out onto the stage to introduce me, and I realized I'd soon be walking away from everything, though I didn't know I'd be leaving with the man I'd sat with in the hotel lobby the night before. That realization only came later in the day, in Sergej's room. I was sitting on the windowsill in the half-light, trying to make out the contours of a hill, as I remembered now while I watched Tome and his wife sitting in silence in their car. Sergej had come out of the bathroom, turned to me, sat on the bed, and taken off his clothes. He placed his hands on his knees, watching me with his waxy face, a little tired, as if to say, "We've come this far, and now we have to go on together." I sat next to him. The tattoo on his chest showed a complex root system reaching all the way up to his neck and shoulders. I traced one of the lines with my finger. "Where's the tree trunk?" I asked. "When you upend the roots, the trunk won't grow," he answered. I

BEDBUGS 173

undressed and put my clothes next to his on the floor. With his finger he circled my right nipple, then placed his hand over it, tenderly, as if checking my breathing. That's what did it, Hladna, the way he touched me, the painless way he entered me. This wasn't a version of love, no, the tenderness of love is different, pained with inner conflicts, because tenderness comes from death—which is the absolute tenderness—no, this was respect for the body, respect entirely pure, with no amorous intentions, much like sympathy. It had to do with lightness. I felt as if I could go with him only in a body that was light, without the weight of identity. And I went. Now, a year and a bit after the crash, I watched the highway and surrounding landscape, trying to remember precisely where it was we had pulled off the highway onto the old road. The sky clouded over and the greenery, still quite sparse, had acquired a grayish tinge. Panties, snacks, the dark, the hospital—this was all I could summon. Remember, Gorana, I told myself, reading the signs along the road. If only I'd kept my eyes fixed on them. If only I hadn't noticed the moment when Tome's wife made a particular move. She ran her left hand, you see, along the inside of Tome's right arm, encircled it and stroked it briefly. A simple sign of simple intimacy. So why did this upset me so deeply? I'll tell you, Hladna, but later, because during the moment when I was watching the tanned arm of Tome's wife, I didn't yet grasp what was disturbing me about what I was seeing. All I felt was that I didn't want to be seeing it, that this had something terrible to tell me. We arrived in Zagreb a little after noon. They dropped me off on Srebrnjak, in front of my landlord's house. I stood there under the cold gray bars of the wall and mustered my courage.

It's over, Gorana, I thought. Now the time has come for you to find out what you're facing. I turned a few times to walk away, but finally pressed the buzzer. There was an electronic gurgle and then the familiar quick voice of my landlord. "Who's there?" I said nothing. "Who's there?" "Gorana Hrabrov, here," I said with difficulty. Silence. "Gorana," he said, as if he needed a moment to remember who I was. "Wait, I'll be right down." For a few minutes the house was silent, too dark and so stern that even the wood-built sections seemed cold. When the front door opened, I could see him through the bars. He seemed relaxed, in a sweat suit and slippers. He opened the door to the yard and looked me up and down, from head to toe. "What do you need?" he asked, not without kindness. I looked at him: in his gray eyes and on his head, smooth as ice, there was no fire. He watched me, questioningly, a little curious. I felt confused. I couldn't remember what I needed. "Has something happened?" he asked. "No," I murmured, "everything's fine. Did you call me down at my sister's place about six months ago?" His face wrinkled up in surprise. "I can't recall," he said. Then it hit him, "Oh, yes, yes, I was trying to find the phone number of your neighbor, Ivica, I needed something urgently." I grinned. "What's so funny?" "Nothing," I said. "Oh, yes, now I remember. I need the spare key, I forgot mine in the apartment." Again, he looked me up and down and then went in to fetch it. I put the key in my bag, said goodbye, and walked down Srebrnjak to Kvaternik Square. I felt every beat of my heart. There was no fire, pounded in my head, it never happened. Maybe I should have been glad, but I felt only emptiness, as if my body were an empty hall with my heart rattling unpleasantly around inside it. The city seemed empty. Vlaška was unusually quiet for an early Saturday afternoon. Everywhere, glued to the doors of the sealed shops and cafés, fluttered notices about COVID-19. Austro-Hungarian edifices, gray under the grayish sky, heightened the lifeless impression, but they also displayed some of their remarkable gentility, as if they, freed from scrutiny, had acquired a nobility that comes with age. Zagreb in the spring is far more beautiful a city than it is in the winter, don't you think? You'll say, every city is. Well, no, some don't benefit from the exposure spring light brings, but Zagreb is protected by its parks and tree-lined avenues, the generous treetops blocking the sun from revealing its architectural infelicities. I walked across the nearly vacant square and along utterly quiet Tkalčićeva. There was nobody in the courtyard on Medveščak. Even the witnesses are gone, I thought, and now I really am completely alone. Unlocking my door, I stepped into the apartment. Months of stagnant air hit me. The broken table lamp lay where it had been; the candle on the desk had melted into the shape of a wax plate. I tossed the keys into my purse, tossed the purse onto the table in the kitchen, and sat down. How to describe for you encountering that space again? Like running into a person whom you'd thought was dead. The walls and furniture, my things and the wilted plants—everything felt so familiar, yet so unreal. I stared at the red rope bowl in which the bananas were small, twisted, and totally black. Before my eyes, I kept seeing Tome's wife's hand as it ran along his arm and encircled it. I paced. Drank a lot of water. Sat on the couch. Checked the bedroom. Then came back to the kitchen table. And then I remembered, Hladna. Oh, yes. I saw my own left hand quite clearly as it ran along the inside of Sergej's right arm and encircled it. Not long before, I'd taken off my panties and tossed them into the trash in the gas station bathroom, and his fingers found their way to my crotch, slid under the woolen dress and over my nylon stockings to my clitoris. I felt their weight. No longer did this have the lightness of that first touch. Now his was the touch of someone who insisted on being my husband. I saw quite clearly how I encircled and clasped his arm in a tight embrace. Too tight. Around the kitchen I paced. Too tight, Hladna, this was too tight a clasp for it to be well-meaning. Into my mind's eye came fast flashes of his last gaze, in which I could discern no dark understanding of any kind. Only the sudden fear of being faced with what was about to happen. I couldn't clearly visualize what I did then with the bag of mixed nuts, but I know what I did. Though my whole mind fought against the thought. And now, as I write this, I want to believe that my clasp was only partly what caused the crash, a mild distraction; there must have been something else, something on the road that spun the steering wheel out of control. How could I, after all, or so my mind protested, bash his face with the bag if he did manage to look over at me? He was stronger than me, said my mind, he could have jerked his arm back in time. But my ear registered, and still registers, the crinkling of the cellophane, the glassy cling of his breath on the silvery interior of the little bag, my right hand over his left hand that was fighting to push me away. Panties. Snacks. The hand. The gaze. The cellophane. The dark. The hospital. I saw you, Hladna, when I came to. You were lying on the bed next to mine, petite and dark-haired, hooked up to equipment that so naturally suited your cold presence that you looked like one big device, a tangle of cables and tubes. The nurses told me you were a young doctor who, like me, had just been through a bad car crash. The two of us lay there alone for nights with the quiet electronic descriptions of our bodies, and for a long time I talked to you, as you know, about myself and you said nothing. Now I can admit this to you: I was sorry my injuries weren't as serious as yours, because I was afraid to be released. I was horrified by the day when I would have to leave you and resume my life. As if I realized that a little over a year later, I'd be sitting in my kitchen, staring at the red rope bowl, and my lower jaw would be shaking so hard, my teeth could be wearing down at high speed, and soon I'd have only gums left. The rope, I thought, looking at the silver anchor on the thick red rope forming the bowl, this rope had been in my house the whole time, on a bowl I'd made myself. I knew it could be pulled off from the wooden base it was glued to and could easily be pried apart with a knife, so I did that. I put it in my bag. I went out. I was guilty, drummed in my head, I killed a stranger who was trying to be my husband. I, who couldn't bear the way he had suddenly become difficult, dragging me down with his full weight, down into reality, down to the place where I was born, down to my mother, who was having difficulty dying in her difficult body. I walked up over Mlinarska Street to the Upper Town and then descended on the other side into Tuškanac Park. Again, I was in a frame of mind where my body was doing things driven by its own automatism, with no thought. When I came out onto the park by Krležin Gvozd, something in me changed. I was still seeking, in all honesty, a tree to hang myself from, but by then I was doing this with shame. You're ridiculous, I berated myself. How are you going to hang yourself with this thin, short length of rope? Parks, I confess, have power over me. For me they are the highest urban authorities. Places where nature shows its concern for a person, where plants, sympathetic toward our brief, troubled lives, consent to be enslaved to free us from our fears. In parks, a person shares a bench with her death. I sat, choosing a place where the passersby, few and far between, wouldn't come near. An uncomfortable north wind, which had been blowing all day, subsided, and then a nice moment of harmony occurred. The milky-white light filtered tenderly through the branches with the first leaves, and the grass acquired a greener hue. The shrubs of white flowers, whose name I couldn't remember, gave off an appealing fragrance. Bees and tiny flies glimmered like sequins. I was indebted to this beautiful landscape; this complex scene made my living senses possible after billions of years of the universe's workings. I sat there like that for a long time, several hours perhaps, until dark. Around eight, I went back to Medveščak, cold and hungry. I threw my bag on the floor and plopped on the couch without taking off my coat or sneakers. Thoughts raced through my mind, but nonetheless, at one point I did drop off to sleep. Architects appeared in my dream. Senenmut the Egyptian, Hadrian the Roman, Daniel Libeskind. The places where I'd been also appeared—Anica's kitchen at dinner, Kiddo's after dinner, Jakovčević's for dinner, the house on the island, Zvijezda's red living room, the apartment on Medveščak—but the same scene kept repeating: the doorbell rings and a woman enters, dressed like a tourist, always with the same face, which I sometimes recognize as Gaudí the architect, sometimes as Adolf Loos, Louis Sullivan, or Viktor Kovačić, and the woman says, "Why sit here, wasting time? You must come with us to build the city." I shake my head. "I can't," I say. "First I have to build myself a house." Then come Bramante, Michelangelo, Walter Gropius, Drago Ibler, Ludwig Mies van der Rohe, Bruno Zevi, Kenzō Tange, Marko Vidaković, Sir Norman Foster, Tadao Ando, Stjepan Planić. "You must build the city," they say. "No, no," I protest, "I don't yet have a house." The woman looks like Zaha Hadid. Her warm, dark eyes watch me. "Come build a city," says Elena's raspy voice, and she proffers a hand. I feel like I'm crying. My throat tightens, and it takes a lot of effort for me to get out a single word. "You don't know how hard it is to be without a house," I say. Zaha sits with me in the kitchen on Medveščak and cries; then she quietly leaves. I turn out the light and remain alone in the dark. Silence. Then I hear them. The patter of billions of tiny ants' feet. I feel them wriggling in the dark, clustering in dense rows, louder and louder and louder, terrifyingly loud, as loud as thunder or the sundering of walls. Someone was banging on my door. "Neighbor!" called a man's voice. "Are you alive?" It took me a few minutes, Hladna, to realize I was actually awake. "Neighbor!" shouted the voice of my neighbor with the half-drooping eyelid. "Are you okay?" "I'm alive," I called. I looked around. In the semidarkness, there were jagged cracks running across the walls. One of the pictures lay smashed on the floor, the other table lamp had also fallen over, drawers had opened, the wardrobe tilted dangerously. I got up and looked out the window into the courtyard. The chimney had fallen onto one of the parked cars; there were roof tiles and chunks of plaster strewn everywhere. Some of the neighbors were already down there. "Earthquake," I whispered. Will you believe me if I tell you, despite the trembling of my legs, that I felt a relief I hadn't felt in years? I went into the bathroom, splashed my face, brushed my hair, and brushed my teeth. I changed into my favorite red cashmere dress and leather knee-high boots, donned my own coat, my gray woolen cap, and my plaid scarf and gloves, and picked my bag up off the floor, and out I went. The morning was very cold, and a light snow was starting to fall. Wan and rumpled, my neighbors eyed each other over their antivirus masks. I put my scarf over my mouth and waited. One of the neighbors, a short woman with big hips, came over to me and said, "Now you architects will have a heyday. What do you think, neighbor, why did everything collapse like it did?" "Because," I said calmly, "Zagreb was built on a lie. Neoclassicism as a style emerged at the behest of early capitalism to conceal its true nature, and the lie has survived until this very day. Zagreb had to come tumbling down sooner or later, because people who are fearful live behind those noble facades." Did I smile? Could she tell? She looked at me as if I were a madwoman and stepped back, at a loss for words. I watched them all together, these neighbors of mine. The widow from the third floor of the street building, who, as always, knew everything and was ordering everybody around, was dressed as neatly as usual, her black hair still motionless like a wig. The groggy gamer from the second floor looked more or less like he always did. There were three different families with teenagers, dressed in whatever they could lay their hands on. I hadn't had much contact with them over the last five years. The young couple who lived on the first floor of the courtyard building was already prepared to move. Well-dressed, wearing rubber gloves and face masks, they stood before a pile of bags, suitcases, and two computers, and were trying to arrange for transportation. The old folks from the apartment beneath mine were lounging on chairs as if they were on a summer terrace, and their granddaughter, a pretty little brown-haired girl of about ten years old, hopped around, pestering them. The three people from India on the first floor of the street building huddled by their entrance. The neighbor whose car had been flattened by the chimney rubbed his eyes with the thumb and forefinger of his right hand, and his two messy little dogs scampered around, out of control, biting the first buds on the stunted forsythia bushes and battling clumps of grass. Most everyone was staring at their phones. News was coming in about the damage, the injuries, the young girl who died on Đorđićeva Street. Someone claimed predictions of a new tremor in twenty minutes. From one of the phones barked a man's voice, ordering people to go out onto the streets and squares. "Don't panic!" shouted the voice. "Proceed to an open area and maintain social distancing!" There was another tremor after 7 a.m. that sent a few more roof tiles flying off both roofs. Everyone crowded into the middle of the courtyard, and the girl from the first floor, who had been quite calm until then, indeed almost festive in her pink coat and little polished boots, screamed and began sobbing. On the walls of both buildings, I could see deep cracks, and gaping holes covered more than half the surface of the roofs. It was clear that people could no longer live there. I stood in the middle of the courtyard, upright, as if on guard, clutching my bag with both hands, and waited. My feet were frozen, my stomach ached with hunger, I shivered from the cold flakes that were falling on my face and neck, but I didn't budge. After ten or eleven, the sky began to clear. By then the neighbors were standing in larger groups, nearer to each other. Someone made coffee; someone brought out bottles of šljivovica and jeger, plastic glasses, Griotte chocolate-covered cherries, Domaćica cookies, and milk chocolate. The platinum-haired woman who always passed by me scowling, without a hello, beckoned me to join them. I shook my head. But I couldn't help noticing what the sun did to them. How the bright light made their skin look both darker and more translucent, much like a brittle, hornlike carapace, how their hair and nails shined mercilessly, how they moved with a certain blind persistence. And the sweetish smell of blood that came from their mouths. Hladna, I saw them here before me in the clear light of day, finally ousted from their hiding places, from the warm beds and cupboards, from the cracks in the parquet flooring and the skeletons of old armchairs. Bedbugs. I was more similar to them, you know, than I'd thought till then, prepared to do anything to survive. Capable of clutching at each momentary little worry, cold feet, a stomach grumbling with hunger, the place where I'd be sleeping the next night, the ground that was still shaking, so I could forget I'd once killed a man with a little bag of mixed nuts. Capable of believing that my memory, as the only witness, must be tricking me. I don't want to say I was no longer thinking about it; indeed, during this last month spent living in temporary accommodation, in a little single bedroom in a student dorm, I am constantly thinking about all sorts of things, and I ask myself questions such as: It's clear I'd been trying to kill myself, but was Sergej merely a case of collateral damage? Or was my desire to free myself from the burden of a husband so strong that I was prepared to sacrifice myself as well? Or did I genuinely believe I'd seen a dark acquiescence in his eyes? How will I move on after all this? Will I ever succeed in building the "ideal house"? Or is there even such a thing as an ideal house? Isn't every house a badly executed idea, a perfect design destroyed by the imperfect lives of those who enter it? I wonder, but downfall, though freeing, offers no answers, no answers whatsoever. The top of the tree I see outside my window is merely the lush top of a tree. The birds that gather in it sing for themselves, not for me. The red Ford Puma, my sole remaining piece of property, is parked in the garage, and each day it loses value. And then again, I think, if I hadn't been able to save the space, perhaps there is also success in the fact that I tamed the fear inside the walls of my body, and my body became my house. Maybe that was what I needed to overcome my horror at the architecture others have built and to move on, with small steps, toward rebuilding the city. Hladna, my dear, no doubt I'm boring you with so many pointless questions. You probably have already fallen asleep next to your empty bottle of pelin and haven't read even half of what I wrote. Or, yes? I keep forgetting that I have no idea whether you ever regained consciousness and were released from the hospital, whether you survived. Are you breathing? Or is this my breath, full of the guilt that I'm slowly growing accustomed to? Hladna, you are Schrödinger's cat, both dead and alive, and I may be writing to you in vain. But, isn't every act of writing futile? Futile, horrible, and the only option. Like life.

About Sandorf Passage

SANDORF PASSAGE publishes work that creates a prismatic perspective on what it means to live in a globalized world. It is a home to writing inspired by both conflict zones and the dangers of complacency. All Sandorf Passage titles share in common how the biggest and most important ideas are best explored in the most personal and intimate of spaces.